PENGUIN BOOKS

KOWLOON TONG

Paul Theroux was born and educated in the United States. After graduating from university in 1963, he travelled first to Italy and then to Africa, where he worked as a Peace Corps teacher at a bush school in Malawi, and as a lecturer at Makerere University in Uganda. In 1968 he joined the University of Singapore and taught in the Department of English for three years. Throughout this time he was publishing short stories and journalism, and wrote a number of novels. Among these were *Fong and the Indians*, *Girls at Play* and *Jungle Lovers*, all of which appear in one volume, *On the Edge of the Great Rift* (Penguin, 1996). In the early 1970s Paul Theroux moved with his wife and two children to Dorset, where he wrote *Saint Jack*, and then on to London. He was a resident in Britain for a total of seventeen years. In this time he wrote a dozen volumes of highly praised fiction and a number of successful travel books, from which a selection of writings were taken to compile his book *Travelling the World* (Penguin, 1992). Paul Theroux has now returned to the United States, but he continues to travel widely.

Paul Theroux's many books include *Picture Palace*, which won the 1978 Whitbread Literary Award; *The Mosquito Coast*, which was the 1981 *Yorkshire Post* Novel of the Year and joint winner of the James Tait Black Memorial Prize, and was also made into a feature film; *Riding the Iron Rooster*, which won the 1988 Thomas Cook Travel Book Award; *The Pillars of Hercules*, shortlisted for the 1996 Thomas Cook Travel Book Award; *My Other Life: A Novel*; *Kowloon Tong*; and *The Collected Stories*, a collection of his short fiction. Most of his books are published in Penguin.

BY PAUL THEROUX IN PENGUIN

Fiction
Waldo
Saint Jack
The Black House
The Family Arsenal
Picture Palace
World's End *
The Mosquito Coast
The London Embassy
O-Zone *
My Secret History *
Chicago Loop
Millroy the Magician
On the Edge of the Great Rift (*containing* Fong and the Indians,
Girls at Play *and* Jungle Lovers)
My Other Life: A Novel
Kowloon Tong

Short stories
The Collected Stories

Travel
The Great Railway Bazaar
The Old Patagonian Express *
The Kingdom by the Sea
Sunrise With Seamonsters *
Riding the Iron Rooster *
The Happy Isles of Oceania
Travelling the World
The Pillars of Hercules

* Not available in the USA

PAUL THEROUX

KOWLOON TONG

A NOVEL

PENGUIN BOOKS

PENGUIN BOOKS

Published by the Penguin Group
Penguin Books Ltd, 27 Wrights Lane, London W8 5TZ, England
Penguin Putnam Inc., 375 Hudson Street, New York, New York 10014, USA
Penguin Books Australia Ltd, Ringwood, Victoria, Australia
Penguin Books Canada Ltd, 10 Alcorn Avenue, Toronto, Ontario, Canada M4V 3B2
Penguin Books (NZ) Ltd, 182–190 Wairau Road, Auckland 10, New Zealand

Penguin Books Ltd, Registered Offices: Harmondsworth, Middlesex, England

First published by Hamish Hamilton 1997
Published in Penguin Books 1998
9 10 8

Printed in England by Clays Ltd, St Ives plc

'*Mah jiu paau*
mouh jiu tiuh'

'The horses will go on running
The dancing will continue'

    – Deng Xiao-ping's pledge,
    in Cantonese, to Hong Kong

ONE

Some days Hong Kong seemed no different from the London suburb she had lived in before the war. Today, for example, the cold early morning with fragments of fog at the windows, she was back in Balham. The gray sky was falling in big soft wisps of tumbled stuffing like a cushion torn open – but not one of those stinky straw-filled Chinese cushions. When the wind gusted the drops of rain, as though flushed from just above her, plopped harder on the roof, which was also the ceiling of the parlor at Albion Cottage. The sky, the roof, the ceiling – on a wet day like this they were one thing.

Betty Mullard sat in what she called the lounge waiting for her son Bunt to come in to breakfast.

'Fancy that,' she said softly to the plip-plop of the rain. 'Chinky-Chonks.'

And she went on thinking: *Chinese relatives? What Chinese relatives?*

She had just put the phone down after speaking to Monty, who was Mr Chuck's solicitor, and also hers – theirs, the firm's, everyone trusted Monty. He was a Londoner too, a lad, sported a bowler hat, and he just laughed and looked at her with dead eyes when she said, 'I trust you because you're a Jew-boy.'

Mr Chuck had never mentioned Chinese relatives.

The question was, How to tell Bunt?

Hearing another sudden clatter of raindrops she was back in Balham again. She looked up and saw the Queen, the portrait over the mahogany sideboard, a larger photograph than that of Betty's late husband George, in his R A F uniform on the same wall. The portrait had been part of the room, as permanent a fixture as the lamps and candle brackets, but lately Betty had begun to look closely at the Queen's face, querying it. The Queen was practically a goddess, but she was also a mother, and a ruler. Her kingdom was established and serene and orderly. 'She works so hard,' was all Betty had ever said, a kind of benediction.

The greatest change Betty had known in her life, keener than the death of her father, worse than the war but with the same unexpected surprises and hurts (all her sighs of 'Whatever next!'), was the seismic shift in the domestic life of the Royal Family. Her father had been old and sick: his time had come. The war had been won. But in these past years Betty had felt a sense of overwhelming disillusionment – loss and grief and bewilderment of an almost blaspheming sort that had very nearly unhinged her – at the news of divorces and muddles and adulteries and scandals and secrets of the Royal Family. Her Majesty excepted, they were human and horrible, and they were naked, exposed for all the world to see. For the first time in her life she saw their flesh, the common freckles on Fergie's moo-cow face, Diana's skinny arms, even Charles's, his white legs. To Bunt, who had no idea of the majesty of the Queen and how much had changed, his mother said, 'And the youngest – just a shame – he's a nancy boy, no question.'

The rain shaken from the overhanging trees fell noisily on the cobbles out front and on the crazy paving that George and Wang had put in. Betty looked in that direction too when she heard the loud dribbling spatter of the drizzle, and she saw the lily cluster, big leaves hit by the falling rain;

nodding, the blossoms seemed to grieve like girls in white bonnets, to share her sorrow.

In her purple woolly jumper Betty matched the tea-cosy that lay thick on the contours of the teapot before her, and the egg-cosies, two of them, that sat on the soft boiled eggs like bobble-hats. On mornings like this Wang always fitted the items with these accessories that Betty had made. The color was unfortunate but it had been cheap, bought in bulk through one of the company's wholesalers, which explained the amount of yarn. There were also purple coasters for the souvenir glasses on the sideboard, where they stood with the souvenir saucers and the letter-holder and the sturdy thermos flask and the tiny ceramic wine barrel from Spain with its clutch of toothpicks, and the various items (brass jar, crystal bear, enamel ashtray) she had bought in the gift shops of transit lounges on her London flights.

With the same wool she had made cuffs for the chairs and collars for the lamps, and the pictures too – of George and Ivy in Carshalton, of Reeny and Ken, and Bunt in his pram at Southend, of an odd foursome, mothers and sons on the beach at Silver Mine Bay in Lantau: Betty and little Bunt with Jia-Jia and her small son Wang – the frames had purple knitted sleeves. They held the damp and filled the lounge with the smell of clammy wool. And cold toast and bacon fat and the savory sourness of just-sliced papaya – Wang had left the kitchen door ajar.

Albion Cottage was off Lugard Road on a bluff above the Peak Fire Station. The fire brigade was inside today, with the windows and doors shut. No voices, no music, no sirens. Everything in the bungalow on a morning like this had a film of dampness, and the dampness seemed to liven the mildew and gave the interior the ripe cheesy odor of a mortuary. Varnished wood was affected, a dampness dulled the case of the wind-up clock with its ponderous ticking and its iffy mainspring; caused a slick on the oak canteen of silver cutlery with its small silver plate, engraved *George and Betty, 1946*; on the newly twisted mechanical calendar that needed a turn every day, reading *THU 7 MAR 96*; the sofa and the needlepoint cushion covers; and the leather footstool (still showing Ted's heelmarks) and the jam jars and the tea tray and the old magazines stacked beside the armchair, and the armchair itself – it all ponged.

Yet on a clear morning, like a hallucination from the east-facing windows, where heavy with blackflies and aphids there were nasturtiums tumbling from a window box, Betty could see China – Red China, as they used to call it. Shum Chun was an hour by train from the factory in Kowloon Tong across the harbor. In forty-five years she had never visited, nor had George when he was alive, nor had Bunt, for – near or far – what was the point in going to China?

Bunt came in blowing his nose, saying, 'Did you hear the phone ring at six o'clock? Imagine a twit calling that early!'

Wang hurried after him, with the toastrack and a plate of bacon, the papaya she had smelled and a napkin bundle.

Bunt folded his handkerchief into his pocket and went to the table and hesitated. He was forty-three and balding, and he touched his scalp lightly with Braille-reading taps and tracings of his fingertips, as though for luck, or searching for hair – or was it perhaps a reflex from the time he had had hair?

'Wang made some fresh oaties. Have an oatie, Bunt. Give him an oatie, Wang, there's a good chap.'

There was an element of pride in Betty's encouragement. It was not really Wang's food. She had taught the man her own recipes and so it was her food.

Wang was tall – taller than Bunt, with a broad north China face, and a flattish head and wide-apart eyes that gave him a snake's features. He looked even more snake-like when he smiled, but that was seldom. His laughter was more frequent but even more sinister – since it never indicated pleasure, only anxiety and fear. He seemed to be on the verge of laughing this morning. Had he heard anything of the phone call?

Wang said nothing. He put the food on the table and withdrew. He had a sloping sideways walk which Betty blamed on his height. He was solitary. He was not mysterious. He jogged.

Bunt said nothing, either. He was dealing with his egg, his mouth was full, there was a fleck of egg on his cheek.

'There's a wee scrap of bacon going spare,' Betty said.

'If it's going spare.' Bunt motioned with his spoon.

'I'll do the honors.'

His mother slid the three stiff rashers onto his plate and then switched on the radio. It was green-painted bakelite with a yellow illuminated dial, as big as a bread bin, and it crackled. George had bought the radio. 'It's a pup,' Betty said, but Bunt still boasted about it for its not being Japanese. It was a Roberts. Like the sturdy John Bull thermos flask on the sideboard it was English-made. 'We manufactured radios once!' The TV was a Bush. The gramophone was a Bush. The toaster was a Dualite. The bathroom porcelain, basin, bath and WC, were all Twyford Adamants. 'And cars.' The Mullards' car was a black 1958 Rover that George had bought. He was proud of all these because, he said, though they might need repair they would never need to be replaced in his lifetime. George was fond of saying – whether of the appliances or his sturdy clothes – 'These will see me out.'

The sounds the Roberts made were like those of an old dear who had had to learn a new language. This morning it was saying, *In the run-up to 1997 –*

The Hand-over: they called it the Chinese Take-away, and it was now the old refrain. It was the only news in Hong Kong – and news related to it, the economy, land reclamation, sales of commercial property, the price of petrol, the new airport, the noisy fears of anxious politicians, all of it was tied to the Hand-over. Because it was the same every day and had been for so long, Bunt never commented. Besides they had vowed they were going to stay, just to see. There was no risk. They had British passports. And they were not so free as others in the colony, for they had a half-share in the factory; the other half belonged to Mr Henry Chuck.

'You'll want your UK woolly,' Betty said. It was one she had made. 'And don't forget your gamp.'

Anticipating that Bunt would say 'Soldiers, Mum?', meaning bread fingers, Betty was buttering bread. She did it her usual way, standing with her feet apart, holding the whole loaf and spreading the butter on the end. When the buttering was complete, she worked her knife through it and cut off the buttered end as a slice. But as she did this Bunt was wagging his finger, no, no, no, because his mouth was full, his cheeks bulging with tea.

Sensing that he could not deny it, Betty said, 'You're nid-nodding over your food. You look a little peaky.'

She knew she would not get the truth from him, but she was curious to know what his lie would be. She watched him closely as he swallowed. She had kept track of what he had eaten: a soft-boiled egg, five rashers of streaky bacon, an oatie, half the papaya, two slices of toast, to one of which he had added jam; no soldiers.

Bunt's reaction this morning was not to lie or make an excuse but to smile and pluck his umbrella from the stand and say he had to go.

'You were late last night,' his mother said, trying to provoke a lie.

6

Bunt smiled and said, 'Cricket Club. Had a drink with Mr Chuck.'

It was the worst lie he could have told, but perhaps it did not matter what he said. The scent of cheap perfume was a hairy cat-like odor of a sluttish woman in her nose when she put his shirt into the laundry basket. If she asked he would only deny it, but who was she? This was Hong Kong – she might be anyone, and that was alarming.

Bunt had gone thrashing into the rain and started the car. He was chafing some warmth into his hands and releasing the handbrake of his black lumpy Rover. He looked up and opened his mouth wide when he saw his mother coming towards him, buffeted by the wind and drizzle. She put her face and her lank rain-flecked hair against the passenger's side window.

'Mr Chuck's dead,' she said.

It sounded like an afterthought, though it was anything but. The news had been worrying her since six o'clock when Monty called. She simply did not know how to tell her son of the death of their business partner.

Though Bunt was not superstitious he knew that thereafter, every time he hitched forward on the leather seat of the old Rover and released the handbrake – or perhaps even gripped it – he would think of those words. The satisfying lift and click to free the mechanism would always be linked in his mind with Mr Chuck's death. He thought of death in the same way – the brakes are off, for that was how it seemed.

'I'm sorry,' Bunt said. 'I didn't really see him at the Cricket Club.'

Betty made a face – twitching eyes, pursed lips – that meant *Never mind*.

She said, 'Evidently he didn't have an earthly –'

His mother was still talking but he was no longer listening.

7

There was too much to do. Instead of the closely regulated schedule of the factory, Imperial Stitching in Kowloon Tong, the entire day had to be improvised. Bunt was someone who hated surprises, even pleasant ones. This was terrible and worse, now everything in his life was in doubt.

And as someone who hated surprises, who was thrown by anything unplanned, or simply not having a plan, an English loathing for improvisation, urgency made him anxious and inaccurate, and hurry left him speechless. Yet the death demanded his attention, and at the end of the day Bunt was astonished by what he had managed to accomplish at such short notice.

He arranged for the funeral service at St John's Cathedral, on Battery Path Road – Mr Chuck, though Chinese, was a devout Anglican; Miss Liu at the factory took care of the flowers, and Mr Cheung the insertion of the death notices in all the papers, including the Chinese ones. Mr Woo lowered the Union Jack on the roof of the factory to half-mast. Lily, Miss Liu's assistant, faxed some dates and club names to the *South China Morning Post* for their obituary. Bunt spent almost an hour at the Hong Kong Club with Monty, the solicitor. By late afternoon, Bunt felt he knew Mr Chuck a great deal better. Apart from his father's death – but he was young then, just eleven – this was his first proper funeral. He realized that death produced unexpected revelations.

They believed they knew the Chinese, he and his mother, knew them especially well because they knew Mr Chuck and Wang so well. The Chinese were frugal first of all, but not mean; they were self-denying and Spartan, strangely cheese-paring and given to binges – also capable of going mental and throwing an entire fortune away at Happy Valley or Sha Tin. In the casinos of Macao they were melancholy and self-destructive. They might seem stern the rest of the time but it was shyness, which was another reason they didn't look you in the eye. They could be sentimental, they did not shed tears – they had much to blub about and that was probably the reason they didn't. They could be tasteless, for frugality was the enemy of fashion. They did not care, they did not complain, they were totally predictable.

Whoever said the Chinese were enigmatic might have met one Chinese person but had not met two. They were nearly always the opposite – obvious, unsubtle, unambiguous, and what was the opposite of mysterious? They carried on their lives in whispers and their business in shouts. If they wanted you to accept a present they rammed it down your throat and the present was never an expensive thing. They liked simplicity more than ingenuity, because ingenuity cost more. But novelty that was a bargain pleased them. Children pleased them, families generally. They hardly drank. They never gave speeches. Patience and long-suffering were attributed to them. No, in Hong Kong they were animated by one emotion and that was impatience. They were not timid – they could fight like cats. They were too shy to say it, but *Hurry up* was the angle and the statement in all their posture.

At the meeting, Monty had said, 'And of course as I told your mother, there are the Chinese relatives to consider.'

And Bunt had raised his face to the man. *Chinese relatives?* Mr Chuck had never spoken of them. He had refused to speak of China at all. That was Chinese – don't look back, don't even think about it. Mr Chuck had come to Hong Kong in 1948 and had started Imperial Stitching with Bunt's father two years later. It was called Imperial Stitching and Labels then. Mr Chuck had never gone back to China. Perhaps that had influenced Bunt in his not going. For many years it had been impossible, then it was difficult, but for the past fifteen years you had the impression that a visit to China was demanded of you. Americans went in their

9

millions – and that convinced Bunt that he would never go, even though he was assured that he could easily manage the trip in his lunch hour.

'I've notified them,' Monty said. 'They will want to do something.'

'I can't imagine what,' Bunt said.

'And if they make demands?'

'They can get stuffed.'

Chinese relatives! Bunt saw himself with a hundred meddling Chinese partners, all named Chuck, in Imperial Stitching.

Mr Chuck's funeral at the Anglican Cathedral of St John's was a solemn affair, attended by the eighty-seven workers from Imperial Stitching, everyone except Maintenance, Mr Woo. Some of them seemed ill-at-ease in the church, others recited the prayers without glancing at the Order of Service.

'We're the only gweilos,' Bunt said.

'And him,' his mother said, facing the pulpit, where Father Briggs stood in his frilly smock preparing to speak.

In his eulogy Father Briggs spoke of Mr Chuck's unselfishness and generosity, and the prosperity he had brought to Hong Kong through the success of the factory. It had started as a modest post-war operation and had risen with the colony. It was now a valuable asset. Each time the Mullards were mentioned by the priest the mother and son frowned so as not to appear frivolous.

'In a very real sense,' the priest intoned, 'Imperial Stitching is the best of British. It is Hong Kong.'

All this while, in the church, surrounded by the Chinese mourners, Bunt was imagining the Filipino girl from last night who called herself Baby, getting on to all fours, naked, and presenting her bottom and looking back at him and saying, 'Let we make some puppies!'

And he laughed remembering that she had pronounced it *fuppies*.

'Bunt?'

He recovered and said, 'Poor Mr Chuck.'

The funeral procession stopped traffic, but at Pok Fu Lam a strange thing happened. Like an apparition rising from between two tenements, twenty hooded figures met the funeral cortège. They were Chinese, but like monks in white cowls – druidical and threatening, pagans ambushing Mr Chuck's Christian burial. Some carried banners with Chinese characters in gold, some banged gongs, some rang bells. One of the banners displayed a picture of a much younger Mr Chuck in a black suit and stiff collar and slicked-down hair. Children also in the stiff white robes carried stacks of fake paper money, like Monopoly money, and small combustible replicas of houses and cars, and wreaths, some like horse-shoes and others like archery targets.

'God help us,' Betty said.

Monty spoke to the driver: 'Hoot at them! Move along!'

These were the Chinese relatives. They mourned noisily, they attached themselves to the big black cars from the mortician's, howling near the hearse and now ringing bells. At the cemetery they burned the tokens and the paper money. They shot off massive red clusters of firecrackers until Pok Fu Lam, the hillside like an amphitheater, was filled with smoke and the smell of gunpowder and the litter from the shredded tissue of cracker wrappers.

And then Mr Chuck's coffin was lowered into the grave, a Christian cross riveted to the lid of his coffin and draped with garlands of flowers, and the Chinese paraphernalia fashioned from red and white paper like a mass of broken kites.

After a week of suspense the will was read at the conference room at Monty's office, at Brittain, Kwok, Lum and Levine, in Hutchison House. Betty and Bunt sat at the oval table, the Chinese relatives crowding around, some sitting, some standing, nearly all of them muttering.

Monty read the will in English, his partner, Y. K. Kwok, translated it into Cantonese. The terms were simple enough. The relatives divided Mr Chuck's personal possessions – books, home furnishings, his collection of exquisite perfume bottles, his Jaguar Vanden Plas. Mr Chuck's cash and 'instruments' (that was the word) went to various Hong Kong charities. Already the relatives were loudly protesting, but there was more. Mr Chuck's share in Imperial Stitching went to Bunt, 'as a tribute to my late partner.' Except for Betty's quarter share, Bunt was sole owner of Imperial Stitching (Hong Kong) Ltd.

On the sidewalk outside Hutchison House, Betty smiled at Mr Chuck's Chinese relatives, most of them silent now, and said, 'Look at them, they're choked.'

TWO

Seeing Bunt was never simple for his mother. He was two people. Just a year before Bunt was born, Betty had lost her new-born son – high fever, chills – the infant Neville they nicknamed Bunt, short for 'Baby Bunting.' She had sung to him,

> Bye, baby bunting,
> Daddy's gone a-hunting,
> Gone to get a rabbit skin,
> To wrap the baby bunting in –

Little Bunt had weakened and died. Betty wept. She said, 'You know you're in a foreign country when they call a runny tummy cholera.' She had come home to an empty crib and the accumulated baby clothes in the 'nursery,' as they had begun to call the boxroom. This was in Bowen Road, where it is crossed by Borrett, their first flat. The nursery held all the visible signs of her preparation and high hopes, and she knew she was pitiable in her husband's eyes. She felt desperate to have a child – and not just another child, but Baby Bunting, she wanted him back. They succeeded within the year and so for forty-three years she usually thought of Bunt as two boys, or else a second child, another Bunt. She knew she would never let him go.

Bunt had a clear memory of the day he was told about the brother who had died.

It was at Happy Valley, a day at the races, he had gone with his mother, the amah's day off – where was Dad? He remembered especially because he was happier than he had ever known. He liked the tram-ride: sitting on the top deck he had seen the grandstand at the racecourse, filled with people. His mother gripped his hand and let him hold the coins for the turnstile at the front of the tram. Though he could not formulate it in words it was an intense feeling – of his mother's attention and effort, her closeness, the warmth of her body; it was love. Later, he watched her call out a horse's name, watched her cheer loudly: she had won. She collected her winnings.

Over tea in the Members' Enclosure she said, 'Bunt, you have to be two people,' and she told him why.

It was so confusing that the boy had his same name, and nickname. As a result, if his mother thought of him as two people he thought of himself as half a person.

His father, George – 'Geo would have got an MBE, at least, if he hadn't of died,' Betty said – had never mentioned that first child, never spoke of the loss. It was not because he was indifferent, or cold, as many people in Hong Kong believed George Mullard to be, but because he was passionate. Beneath his placid and usually unflappable exterior and his cry of 'Mustn't grumble!' was a man who was extremely sensitive and sentimental. His own mother and father had been. He believed that the English took trouble to mask such emotions so as not to be a burden. Americans cried – American men blubbed all the time. George kept himself in check, he made a point of not disclosing his feelings and revealed his emotional side in only the pettiest matters – the price of postage stamps, a belittling remark about the Royal Family, or what he took to be wastefulness. 'There's not a thing wrong with that banana. The dark spots only mean it's ripe.' He opened parcels carefully and smoothed and folded the brown paper, he saved glass bottles and returned jingling crates of them to the brewery, he saved string and was proud of the ball he had made.

String-saving had led him to Mr Chuck, for Mr Chuck also saved string, and one day in Victoria Park rolling a length of string around his hand – the lost tether of someone's kite – he had come face to face with Mr Chuck, who was rolling the same piece of string from the opposite end. 'Snap!' George cried out. Mr Chuck gave his name as Henry. The two men, one English, the other Chinese, laughed at their predicament and their frugality and in that moment, seeing themselves as kindred souls, they became friends.

By then, Wing-Commander G. F. S. Mullard had been demobbed and was simply 'Geo,' a newly married accounts clerk in the shipping department at Jardine's. Mr Chuck had arrived not long before from China – he described himself frankly as a refugee, he was grateful to the colony for allowing him entrance. He was looking for premises to start a textile factory. It was a fantasy of George's to run his own business and indulging this fantasy he had made a note of various vacant buildings in Kowloon. He was able to provide many suggestions and he was fascinated when Mr Chuck acted upon them in such an unusual way. Mr Chuck hired a Chinese geomancer to examine each site. George had expected a scowling man in bright robes with red eyes and a sorcerer's cap. The geomancer was a little smiling man with spiky hair and a rumpled suit and might have been a tram conductor. His name was Mo. In a well-made wooden box he carried a *feng-shui* compass, and this he used to evaluate the sites.

With enthusiasm and obvious skill, sketching on the back of an envelope, he explained the spiritual energy of Hong Kong, the way it was channeled and harmonized. It was a little lesson in divination and when Mr Mo had finished Hong Kong seemed to George a place of marvels. The mountains above Kowloon were nine dragons. Hong Kong itself, detached from the mainland and beautifully shaped, was the dragon's ball.

'You see the *long zhu*? The ball?' Mr Mo was making his map.

They sat in a coffee shop, George and Mr Chuck and Mr Mo, in Mong Kok, where Mr Mo lived.

'We are Sons of the Dragon,' Mr Mo said, scribbling. 'Sons of the Yellow Emperor.'

'The meaning is that we are Chinese,' Mr Chuck said. 'That is all.'

Of all the sites, the one in Kowloon Tong was shown by the geomancer's compass to be right in every way. The *feng-shui*, wind-water, was so harmonious that Mr Mo exclaimed that this spot on Waterloo Road fitted the classical epithet for the perfect Chinese address, 'The Belly of the Dragon'. It was at the edge of the old tong, the pond where in a fabulous age the Nine Dragons had crouched to drink. The small splintery house there, with its dead tree and the buried dog bones – all dark omens – would have of course to be removed. But if the new building combined the Five Elements, and if it had no triangles in it, and was built long and narrow, its narrowness facing north–south on the natural channel of Waterloo Road, that was as effective a conveyor of fluid vitality as a river; and if the red doors had prominent arches over them to allow the passage of that same *Ch'i*, the flow of energy through Kowloon, the structure on this auspicious site would bring good luck and great prosperity. In the raising of the structure the Five Elements were incorporated into the factory building: Earth was its brick, Fire its electricity and red doors, Wood its paneling and beams, Water its mirrors and the tong beneath it, Metal its sewing-machines.

Imperial Stitching started a year later. Mr Chuck put up

most of the money. Using all his savings as an investment, and the promise of his work, George became Mr Chuck's partner. It helped that George was British, too, since Imperial Stitching specialized in uniforms – school uniforms, chauffeurs' jackets, concierges' frock coats, matrons' whites, nurses' smocks – the sort of items the colonial government ordered in large numbers, when George's bid on a government tender got a favorable response. The factory employed two hundred workers, mostly women, and also made shirts and slacks and simple dresses. Mr Chuck bought some machinery in Japan that did elaborate embroidery – names, designs, monograms, name tapes, labels, insignia for club ties and flags, badges of all sorts, and they became Imperial Stitching and Labels (Hong Kong) Ltd. They were well known in the colony for fashioning the complex badges for the breast pockets of English club blazers.

Mr Chuck had fled China in 1948, a year of military defeats. He never spoke of China, he would not listen to anything about it. George Mullard was grateful for being spared descriptions of disappointment and terror and loss. He hated hearing of events which could not be reversed. The factory was new, the friendship was new, there was no shortage of orders. Mr Chuck and Mr Mullard were alike in their unwillingness to look back and, new to Hong Kong, they had a sense of freedom as well as the restless impatience of so many others there in the colony of loose rules and no taxes.

When, a year after Imperial started, Betty lost the child, Mr Chuck said nothing specific, though his sympathy was apparent in everything he did. George silently thanked him for that; he would have found a show of sorrow, or any expression of it, unbearable. He surmised that like him the Chinese man was also too emotional to mention anything so sad as the death of a child. Perhaps he himself had known such a bereavement?

Betty was pregnant again. But that was not enough; she had been pregnant before. The child had to live. Bunt was born – Neville George Mullard – he was healthy, as boisterous as two children. Mr Chuck sent presents, and later in various ways he indulged the boy. They called him 'uncle.' They knew nothing of his personal life. Mr Chuck was apparently unmarried, apparently childless.

The partnership flourished because of the distance, the politeness, the respectful silences. The two men were inquisitive, but they were discreet, and they were courteous, and so they remained friends. Though there was a world of difference between them, the Chinese man, the English man – and they knew it – they also believed they had a great deal in common, and not just the factory but many principles, much sympathy and – something they felt deeply but a word they never used – heart.

Looking on, in knee socks, wearing a school uniform from his father's factory, and carrying a satchel of books, was Bunt. Other children were sent back to England for their education. They talked of going on home leave, of school allowances, of London. But George's business was local. There were no perks, no annual leave, no passages, no pension. That was Hong Kong; he was like Mr Chuck, like so many of the Chinese – he was on his own.

Bunt was taken by his mother on the bus and the tram from home to school, Queen's in Causeway Bay. And the lonely woman met him after school; she waited by the great iron gate in Tung Lo Wan Road, near the iced-lolly seller who sat by his barrow; and she took him home, and watched him have his tea, cooked by his amah, Jia-Jia, served by Jia-Jia's son Wang.

It was an embarrassment to Bunt years later to hear

his mother relate his first words, which were in Hokkien. 'Nee-nee,' he had said, pointing, then clutching with chubby fingers. The word meant breasts. Jia-Jia taught him many other words. She claimed the child was fluent in Hokkien.

'Takes after me,' Betty said, and roared, and coughed. She was smoking then.

Bunt's fears and prejudices were all derived from Wang. Wang hated root vegetables, and black hats, and milk in his tea; he left his shoes outside and wore plastic sandals in the house; he regarded ice in his drinks as unhealthy, he had a hatred of bodily hair and pig fat, certain insects made him ill, though he had no fear of rats. Bunt shared all these feelings, and more. He choked on corn silk, believing it was human hair. Melted cheese he mistook for white fat cut from pig meat and he was sick. He had Wang's horror of maggots, and any odd rice grain provoked his fear and he was violently ill. He was not always such a sad and fearful boy, but often when he was young he looked like a little old man.

When he was very young his father had given him a toy telephone and taught him to dial the emergency number for the police.

'Now say, "I want to speak to a gweilo policeman."'

'I want to speak to a gweiwo powiceman.'

Meeting him after school one day Betty did not take Bunt home, but to the hospital, where his father lay propped on pillows. His father's face was yellow. He gasped, attempting to speak. His fingers were bony and cold when he took Bunt's hand. That night his father died. The funeral service was gloomy and ponderous and confusing – so many strangers, when all Bunt wanted was to be alone. Mr Chuck was there, white-faced, looking stunned. Bunt was eleven years old.

That same week, a race week, Betty took the boy to Happy

Valley. She held betting slips, she watched the horses, but she said nothing. Was she losing?

Over tea Betty said, 'I do wish you would try it with milk, just once,' and then, 'You're not a little boy any more.'

A race was being run; through the seat of his chair Bunt could feel the horses' hooves striking the turf. A plummy English voice, talking very fast, was describing the race. *And coming up on the outside –*

'Now you have to take Daddy's place,' his mother said.

– and in the home stretch –

'You have to be the Daddy now.'

Mr Chuck, loyal in his actions even though he had never said much, resolutely dealt with the death. 'Uncle' was his honorific, but his manner was also avuncular – benign, uncritical, concerned, helpful, practical, loving; attentive to Betty in an almost brotherly way, and towards Bunt like the most tactful stepfather. There was nothing of his Hong Kong manner in his relations towards Betty and Bunt. The man was patient, but Betty trusted him with her son, as she trusted Wang and Jia-Jia. She saw no inconsistency. She still did not like Chinese people, she laughed at them, she said they made her weary, she said 'We're working for them!' and she never stopped calling them 'Chinky-Chonks.'

She could see that Mr Chuck was bringing the boy along. He called him Neville. He served as Bunt's protector. Bunt needed protection. The riots of 1967 were nightmarish – violent, unexpected. Imperial Stitching suffered: orders could not be met. The workers were threatened, some were suspected of having sympathy for the demonstrators, but Mr Chuck, who understood the frenzy, defended them, saying they had been intimidated. The fright passed, though windows had been broken in the building, and slogans painted on the walls at ground level. The disruption had been general – they were not being singled out. Yet the name Imperial Stitching seemed to excite the anger of some demonstrators, turning them into rioters. The sign was pulled down twice, the flag was torn from its pole and set alight in the Waterloo Road.

On earning his School Certificate in 1969, Bunt began to be trained at the factory by Mr Chuck. Bunt knew that he was carrying on his father's work. He did not object. He was used to burdens – there was, after all, his dead brother, whose life he seemed to be living too. Just eighteen, already his hair was growing thin. He was a worried child and then a worried adult, and except for his school friend Corkill he hardly remembered his strange accelerated boyhood.

Hong Kong was rising – more buildings, more roads, more settlement. Every year, Mr Mo the geomancer showed up with his wooden box and took readings with his compass. 'Very good,' he said, pronouncing the *feng-shui* still in excellent balance. Sometimes Mr Mo made suggestions for improvements – directions for moving desks and machines and stools. He said, 'If you want change in your life, move twenty-seven things in your house.' When the viaduct was built, cutting Kowloon in half, Mr Mo said they were saved by their alignment with an overpass. 'A lot of old rope,' Betty said, but secretly she was pleased, treating Mr Mo's readings as compliments. Bunt said nothing because in his heart Bunt believed.

In time, Mr Chuck came to work less and less, and depended on Bunt to run the business. It was not difficult for Bunt: the workers were so responsible, so hard-working and thorough that they needed little supervision. Bunt continued to keep office hours, and he developed yet another life.

Imperial Stitching in Kowloon Tong was near the station – on the main line to Lo Wu, to Shum Chun, to China. He had never boarded that train, but its proximity meant there were many bars and blue hotels in the area. Blue hotels were short-time places, one step up from knocking-shops. There were massage parlors, there were clubs, eventually there were karaoke bars. There were upstairs apartments partitioned into cubicles – you could hear rusty bedsprings oinking in the next stall – called 'chicken houses,' *gai dao*. Bunt knew the expression, and though he could not read a word of Chinese, he easily learned to recognize the black strokes of the four characters hastily painted on the red banner, *sun-dou-bak-mui*, that meant 'New Girl from North,' fresh meat. There were the other places, the self-employed tart working from home: *yet lau, yet feng*, one room, one phoenix. It was legal, because no pimp was involved, just a working girl, a phoenix.

Wang made sandwiches for him. His mother packed them in his lunch box. Bunt ate them in the bars – in the Pussy Cat, and the Lilac Lounge, the Good Time, the Coconut Club, Fat-Fat Chong, Happy Bar, and Jack's Place. Even at noon they were open, and though they were usually empty they were ready for business.

'You want a chicken,' the Mamasan would say to Bunt, as he ate his cheese and pickle sandwiches at the bar. The woman was matter-of-fact, she did not leer, there was no archness in her tone. That helped. A wink or any suggestion of it would have undone him. In the very beginning he had thought she meant food, and he was hungry, he said yes. Upstairs he was too shy to admit his mistake, and so he was helped, panting, his eyes popping, by an experienced woman with skinny thighs. She complimented him on his perform-ance, he was young enough to believe her, and that was his initiation.

Mentioning to the Mamasan in the Pussy Cat who he was – naming Imperial Stitching – she hinted broadly that she had known his father. No one went to such a place casually.

You had to be alert and purposeful, though it was always a mistake to seem so. But his father?

Bunt found a way of mentioning this to his mother. He laughed, he shrugged, he said, 'I don't apportion blame.'

'I do apportion blame,' she said, coughing in her fury. 'He had an eye for the ladies.'

Bunt did not think less of the man. On the contrary, it seemed to him as though in his lunchtime visits to the Pussy Cat and Happy Bar and Jack's Place he might be carrying on a family tradition.

The girls were Chinese, they were Filipino, they were Vietnamese, now and then Eurasians, they were mostly young, they were very pretty, it was so easy. And if you lived with your mother and your mother was Betty Mullard they were a necessity. They made no claims on him, they asked for very little and the Mamasan got more than half. This was not Wanchai or Tsim Sha Tsui, the ridiculous clubs haunted by local gweilos and tourists, over-priced, hurry up, mister, only tree-tousand. This was home.

So, like his father, he had a secret – perhaps the only thing his mother did not know, and this was important to him. It was his only strength. He wanted to tell Mr Chuck, because he suspected that the old man knew anyway – the Chinese said nothing and seemed to know everything – but, as Bunt stumblingly started to confess, Mr Chuck stopped him. He always remembered how Mr Chuck had cautioned him.

'A secret is only a secret if you keep it.' And Mr Chuck smiled.

Years later he understood the man's wisdom. By then he was frequenting the chicken houses and karaoke lounges in Mong Kok, where gweilos never went. The encounters were brief, frantic, hurried, mostly silent, because he had to get back to the office, or back to his mother. And though they were experienced in not showing it, the girls were in a great hurry too.

One day in Kowloon Tong, in the Pussy Cat, Bunt saw Mr Chuck in a back booth, his reflection in a mirror. The girl beside him looked familiar too – she was almost certainly one he had been with. Bunt understood the old man better that day. You could say anything to these girls, or nothing. Down at the Cricket Club he had heard men speaking of bar girls and complaining, 'They have no feelings.' Precisely: that was their greatest virtue, that they made no claims, no demands, had no hopes. They were the happy hello-goodbye of urgent sex. It was not about them, but about your own pleasure. They reserved their feelings for other matters. The workers at Imperial Stitching and Labels – say, one of those pretty girls, Mei-ping or Ah Fu – never said they didn't like the job, nor did they say they liked it; they simply sat down and did it. They were paid, they performed, they were gone, like the girls in the bars. They did the work, they would do almost anything that was asked of them. Their greatest skill was in vanishing at the very end and leaving Bunt to himself. He preferred the simplest, most silent girls. He hated all talk. Humor he felt to be out of place in any sexual encounter. It made him feel self-conscious and silly. He disliked the Filipino girls – whose English was usually good – for attempting jokes.

Mei-ping was so pretty. She was a good worker too. One day she was in his office past quitting time, going over a badge pattern. 'I don't want to keep you.' She had lingered. 'It's okay, mister.' She was seated on his sofa. He left his desk and sat beside her. He touched her, he kissed her. 'Do you like that?' She had said nothing. Nothing meant yes. In that Hong Kong way Mei-ping became one of his lovers.

He succeeded with Mei-ping by treating her like a chicken,

like a phoenix. He expected only that she cooperate, and at the end of it he rewarded her, with money or with a present – she said she preferred presents, he suspected her preference to be money. He tried to keep the other girls in the factory from knowing, but they probably knew – they knew everything. Mei-ping had no family. She said she had come from China some years ago. She lived in a room with the other one, Ah Fu, who was similarly alone. He wanted to make love to Ah Fu too, but he knew it would complicate matters. They would not say when or how they had come from China. They were probably eye-eyes – illegal immigrants – though what did it matter? This was not China, it was a British colony, with the Union Jack flying over the whore-houses and the factories and the bars and the banks and the police stations and Government House.

They were afternoon and early evening affairs, in the hours between work and home, his factory and his mother. Nearly every day of his life he had spent under her roof. They ate every night at Albion Cottage. They rarely went out – they disliked Chinese food and indeed made a point of never eating it. In the years before television they had listened to Armed Forces Radio; and often still did, on the green radio that was as big as a bread bin, that got hot when it was left on.

Betty gambled at Happy Valley and Sha Tin, but never recklessly. 'Just a flutter.' She hedged her bets with what was known at the Hong Kong racecourses as a Quinella, choosing the first and second horse in the same race. She liked sitting in the Members' Enclosure on race days with a plate of chips and her binoculars. Bunt was a member of the Hong Kong Club by virtue of his father's membership; and the Cricket Club, not for the cricket but the bowls. He went to St John's Cathedral. He saw Mr Chuck less and less at the factory, but at least once a month he showed the old man the month's accounts, the orders, the wages bill, the overheads, the revenue.

'Lovely and cool in here,' a visitor had once said to him on the cutting floor. It was a Hong Kong May, the city was stifling. 'Good air-conditioning.'

But there was no air-conditioning. It was just open windows and damp bricks, ventilation and shadows. It was the *feng-shui*, perfect harmony.

Bunt turned forty. He gave up smoking. His father had smoked, so had his mum. A bad month at the factory had him on three packs a day, and soon the skin on his forearms turned as brown as a kipper, and he seemed to be sweating smoky poisons through his pores. His throat was raw, his eyes stung, his fingers were trembly. It was not hard for him to lay off cigarettes for a day – indeed, it made him feel a bit better to desist. But after two days it was an effort of will to fight off the urge to light up. He sucked sweets, he paced, he shouted, he even barked; and he stopped drinking, because alcohol made his craving worse.

He had believed that in the long run giving up smoking would make little difference to his health. But the change was profound and unpleasant – not smoking turned him into someone else, a simpler, fatter, more agitated person, with chronic indigestion. It became a way of dating his life, to before and after smoking. He was smug and took some satisfaction in having quit, but he mourned the loss of his cigarettes. And he suffered.

There was first of all the shock to his system. He was light-headed, he slept badly, his throat ached as though he had been smoking. Without cigarettes he had to learn how to eat again. He had to find new ways to digest food. He was never more constipated than when he gave up, and that never left him. He was much hungrier and each meal ended with an urge to smoke. He ate more instead, he developed a sweet tooth, for almost a year he drank nothing but cream sherry. After a time he was disgusted by the smell of other people's smoke, but he knew that these smokers had inhaled the best of it – the heated sweetness of the toasted leaves – had gulped away the tobacco aromas of roasted nuts and ripe fruit; and what they snorted out of their nostrils was the sour exhaust.

Smoking was a blotter which soaked up time, the minutes of a phone call, the hours between meetings, the meetings themselves. So, without smoking, his days were longer by three or four hours, and having no use for the time – and every minute being aware of the pleasure he was missing in having abandoned tobacco – he spent more hours at the Pussy Cat and Fat-Fat Chong rather than at Imperial Stitching. The decision to quit smoking changed his life and he was never able to say for certain that it had been a change for the better.

Business had been good in the 1950s – but that was hearsay. Bunt's awareness dated from the 1960s, when business had been poor. Orders had picked up in the 1970s, boomed and busted in the 1980s and after a brief recovery most of the factories, textiles especially, had moved to China, relocating just over the border in Guangdong.

Mr Chuck refused to move. Instead he adjusted, approved the cutting of the staff, retooling to make cheaper labels and badges, stopped making shirts, made fewer uniforms – how could he compete with the China-based factories? – and Imperial Stitching and Labels grew smaller. They still occupied eight floors but there was more empty space. The offices were on the top floor, Shipping on the ground floor. Nearby factories manufactured Eddie Bauer and Anne Klein and Donna Karan, some of them made five different brands on the same floor. But Bunt was almost exclusively engaged in making labels and in defiance, with Mr Chuck's permission, he dropped 'Labels' from the company name, changing it to Imperial Stitching.

In 1984, Margaret Thatcher announced the Hand-over of Hong Kong to China. The Chinese had been mentioning it for years, but the British had scoffed. Incredibly, the promise was made.

'It may never happen,' Betty said – one of her sayings, it meant, 'Cheer up!'

But events moved ahead, baffling the Mullards, mother and son, baffling many people they knew – enraging Mr Chuck. It was now inevitable. What had changed? Business was not good but there was money about. Many Chinese had gone to Canada, some had returned. Now they hardly thought about the Hand-over, except when it was boringly described in the newspaper, or ranted about by some politicians. Mr Chuck's heroes were Emily Lau and Martin Lee. Betty refused to think about the Hand-over, she hated all the talk.

'Jeremiahs,' she said. 'It's just Chinese Take-away!'

That was why, when Mr Chuck died, Betty said, 'Maybe it's for the best,' thinking of how upset Mr Chuck was at the prospect of 1997. 'Maybe you could say it was one of those merciful releases.'

THREE

After the two funerals, after the reading of the will, after the departure of Mr Chuck's relatives, after all the urgencies and interruptions of the old man's death – the fuss, the sniveling, the expense – life returned to normal for Betty and Bunt. The soft-boiled eggs at Albion Cottage and the lunch box. Wang's oaties, his dismal fruit salads, his dinners of boiled vegetables and burned meat. Betty's knitting: 'I've got a new color,' she said. 'It's called "graphite."' She was making coasters again. Imperial Stitching resumed with its full work-force and some new accounts. 'Royal' was being dropped from many club and company names, in anticipation of the Hand-over, so new badges and monograms were being ordered. The factory was busy, phones were ringing more often in the office, there was greater noise from the cutting and stitching floors, and the Hong Kong radio in Shipping played meaningless music.

The clammy cold days of early March gave way a week later to humid heat: a taste of the next six months, growing worse by the week, a foretaste of stifling April, monsoon May, suffocating June, and the summer sauna. Bunt liked the bad weather for its being an easy topic of conversation with his mother, and a handy source of excuses for being home late and looking harassed, when the truth was that he had been with a woman in a blue hotel or the back booth of the Pussy Cat.

It seemed remarkable to Bunt that the whole of Imperial Stitching was now his. Yet he felt the pressure of others hovering near him in the enterprise – his dead brother and namesake, his dead father, and now dead Mr Chuck. They guided, they chivvied, they signaled for attention. These ghostly presences were as real to him, and as awkward and demanding as his mother – Betty with her quarter share of Imperial. He was working for them all, as much as he was for himself. They were restless, they allowed him no peace – and he would have welcomed a bit of solitude. Seeing him, club members said, 'You're on your own an awful lot, Neville,' and seemed to pity him. But he was never alone.

About ten days after the reading of the will, Bunt's routine was re-established. He woke at seven, listened to the radio, switched off when the Hand-over news came on, then met his mother in the lounge and had breakfast while she watched. 'And a wee scrap of toast –' He gulped his tea, he filled his mouth with toast, he cracked and lopped off the top of his egg with one sideways hit of his spoon, scraped that bit of cranium clean, then went at it with toast soldiers. He never stopped chewing, he breathed through his nose, and all the while his mother hovered, not eating herself – so it was less a meal than a performance.

Wang went back and forth, from kitchen to lounge, scuffing in his plastic sandals, stacking plates, setting Bunt's teeth on edge. The man's height – he was a little over six feet – was impressive, because it was useless in this job. But what Bunt found himself reflecting on from time to time was that Wang was his own age, which was forty-three. The fact preoccupied him, and sometimes it baffled him. He seldom thought about Wang any more, except when remembering how Wang's mother Jia-Jia had been his amah, and how the man at times had frightened him. But when he did, and compared himself to Wang, Bunt concluded that though they were utterly different in every way, nothing would change for either of them, ever. Their lives were fixed for good as master and servant.

This morning Bunt stood and smacked his lips, while his mother wiped a fleck of yolk from his chin, and then – muttering something about the heat – he remembered Mr Chuck as he released his handbrake, and left in his Rover, driving past the Peak Fire Station, down the long hill and into the tunnel traffic to Kowloon, and all the familiar detours. From home to office he saw nothing. After all these years Hong Kong had become invisible to him, and even when someone pointed out a new hotel or office block, more land reclaimed, another shop, he might look but he saw nothing. The city was no more real to him than the signs, which he could not read, the Cantonese language which was just a grating noise that did not remotely resemble human speech. Up the flyover, to Princess, to Waterloo, and at last he came to rest at a painted stall beside the building, which he had begun to think of as his building.

Mr Woo the janitor said good-morning and stuck his arm into the elevator to hold open the door and punched the top-floor button to save Bunt the trouble. Bunt went directly to his office. Miss Liu brought him a cup of tea and a folder of mail – bills, queries, busybody brochures. 'Hand-over bumf,' Bunt said, and gave those items back to Miss Liu, the schedules and new regulations. 'File it.' He did not want to think about the event. When he was asked his intentions he said, 'I'm staying. Nothing will change,' and most of the time he meant it. Hong Kong was just an ant-hill with a Union Jack flying over it. The flag was changing but Hong Kong would remain an ant-hill.

Where was Mr Cheung? There was no sign of the general manager. They met each morning and went over the orders and the daily objectives. Because of Cheung the factory was well run and orderly, and orders were filled on time. Cheung simply asked for approval – like Bunt, Cheung had been trained by Mr Chuck.

Bunt usually saved his reading of the *South China Morning Post* for his second cup of tea, after Cheung left, but today – untypically – he opened the paper. He skimmed the world news, he skipped the Hand-over news, he settled on crime, which was always unusual and sometimes gripping. Of a page of violent stories, one caught his eye: a man in jail for assaulting and disfiguring his wife was bringing a case against the poor woman because she had refused to sell the family house. Two things interested Bunt about the story. The first was the audacity of the man in suing his wife – his victim; the second was the crime itself. He had accused her of adultery and demanded she leave him. *You must leave, but your face belongs to me*, the man had said, and he had bound her with his neckties and poured acid on her face. *I will take your face away.* So disfigured was she that she had been unable to get a job and she needed the house. She had two children. The violent acid-throwing husband wanted the profit from his half of the house. *Seriously disfigured*, the story said. Bunt wondered what she looked like.

'Excuse me, sir.'

Bunt was so startled for an instant he saw the villain from the newspaper story at his office door.

But it was Mr Cheung, jerking his head and grunting, his way of saying sorry.

'The train was late.'

'What train?'

Cheung lived in Kowloon Tong.

'This morning I went to China,' Mr Cheung said.

'Fancy that.'

To wake up and travel to the People's Republic of China and return before ten the same morning seemed foolish. Bunt told himself that such a journey was so pointless he would not inquire further into the absurdity.

Licking his thumb, Mr Cheung worked his way through a clipboard of orders, and only when he looked up did he realize that Bunt was still staring at him, wondering about the China trip.

'I went to Shum Chun,' Mr Cheung said. 'Then to Dong-guan. You know Dongguan?'

'I don't have the foggiest,' Bunt said.

'Beyond Shum Chun. They make toys. Combs. Everything. Very busy place.'

'How did you manage all that?'

'Train. From here. Kowloon Tong,' Mr Cheung said. 'It is on the main line, eh?'

'If you say so. Nice trip?'

'Bought a flat.'

'Also today?'

Mr Cheung was growing uncomfortable with the questions, but Bunt persisted. He nodded – yes, he had bought the flat today.

'You could have bought one in Hong Kong.'

'Here a flat is millions. In Dongguan a big flat is two hundred thousand.'

Bunt had not lost the habit, acquired from his parents, of translating large sums of Hong Kong dollars into pounds sterling. This was less than twenty-five thousand; for the price of a mediocre Japanese car, Mr Cheung had bought a large place to live in across the border in China.

'Fancy that,' Bunt said, but this time with interest.

As they went over the orders, Bunt continued to stare at the man who had woken up and taken the train to China and bought a flat and returned to Hong Kong just a few minutes late for work. It seemed extraordinary and went on baffling Bunt, even after Cheung returned to the factory floor, and Bunt went back to the newspaper, to re-read the story of the jealous husband. *You must leave, but your face belongs to me . . . I will take your face away*. Another reason not to get married.

'Line one,' Miss Liu said.

'Morning, squire' – Monty, his usual greeting – 'I need your signature.'

'Again?'

'You'd better get used to it, squire,' Monty said. 'There's no end to these papers. It's transfers, see. Be glad it's gone so smoothly.'

'Those Chinese relatives had me rigid.'

'They're back in their box, squire. Not to worry.'

'Where's their box?'

'Chuck's home village – Zhongshan, south of Canton. Sun Yat-sen came from there. Delightful place.'

'If it's so pleasant why did we have to beat Chuck's relatives off with a shitty stick?'

'The lychees you eat? Zhongshan is famous for them – that's where they're grown. And longans. All sorts of fruit.'

Bunt just laughed. His hatred for Chinese food extended to the plants, the fruit, the trees that were native to the country, and the country itself, the whole of it – he had no interest, and he could feel hostile when he felt – as he did now, with Monty on the line – that he was being provoked.

'If any of those relatives had inherited a share of Imperial Stitching you wouldn't be laughing,' Monty said. 'It would be shambolic.'

'Quite right,' Bunt said, and after they agreed to meet at the Cricket Club that evening after work, he rang off.

Another of the management strategies Mr Chuck had taught Bunt was to walk the length of each floor each day at different times and make a show of scrutinizing the workers. The idea was to remind them you were in charge, to make them self-conscious, to keep them alert: you had to be unpredictable and silent and you had to keep them insecure, forever guessing. It did not matter whether Bunt paid attention as long as, every day, he showed up in every department. 'They must see you.' It also helped to examine a label or a garment and contrive an incomprehensible sound, a snort, a provisional snicking in his nose, and move on, without making eye contact.

He was uttering noises at a table in the stitching room when Mei-ping approached him and said shyly, 'I'm sorry.'

It took a moment for him to understand that she was referring to Mr Chuck. He had not seen her since the funeral. He hesitated, he smiled, he thought how pretty Mei-ping was.

His lunch box in his hand, Bunt walked down the road to the Pussy Cat. He ordered a glass of beer, then sat in a booth eating the cheese and chutney sandwiches – Wang had made them, he knew from the careful way the crusts had been cut off. It was early enough at noon for only a few girls to be in the bar, and no other customers. As usual the barman, Wendell, was watching television with his back turned to the bar; and the music in the bar was so loud it drowned out the racing commentary. Wendell did not seem to mind. Though he sometimes spoke to the girls or the Mamasan he seldom returned Bunt's greeting. Usually Wendell watched horse races, but today he was watching a Chinese woman being interviewed. Bunt recognized the shrill voice as that of Emily Lau, a member of the Legislative Council.

– *The British could give us citizenship, but they refuse. Because we are yellow! Yet they give it to Australians and Canadians!*

The Mamasan brought him the bottle of beer and sat with him, holding her cellular phone, while he drank and ate.

Bunt was so well known in the club that nothing was expected of him – the usual drink for the girls, tips for the bartender, a present for the Mamasan. They knew that he was fleeing from his office, and they knew about the death of Mr Chuck; at lunchtime he wanted to be left alone. After work, it was another story; they surrounded him and competed for his attention.

– *Yes, there is a lease. But if the lease ends on a flat you return the flat. You don't return the tenants.*

'Wendell, turn the TV down!' the Mamasan shouted. And then she said in a commiserating way, 'Too bad about Mr Chuck.'

How strange it was that he had gotten over it, the factory was his, the grieving had ended; and yet though the sad matter was apparently settled in the minds of others he was continually reminded of the dead man.

Bunt said, 'I saw him in here once.'

The Mamasan nodded. She was plump, Cantonese, with a pink freckly face and her glasses perched on her head. He felt familiar yet awkward with her; she was the woman who had suggested, with facial expressions alone, that she had slept with his father. Now Bunt did not want to know.

Her cellular phone rang. She answered it, and spoke briefly in a tone of giving an instruction, and then she switched it off.

'Bad line,' she said. 'China.'

He remembered Cheung. He said, 'I talked with a bloke this morning who just hared up to China and bought a flat.'

'They are cheap,' the Mamasan said. 'It is so easy from here – just an hour, this train to Shum Chun.'

'That's the place,' Bunt said. 'So your girls go there?'

'Even work there,' she said. 'I send girls to Beijing even. Shanghai, Guangzhou also.'

'Isn't that dangerous?' Bunt said. Because he had never

36

been to China it seemed to him a place of darkness and ambush.

'Yes, dangerous, because girl-business is illegal in China. But the men are powerful. And the money is good.'

'They're not afraid,' Bunt said. 'They'll do anything for that.'

He liked speculating on the word 'anything.' He enjoyed this, eating his cheese and chutney sandwich and his pickle and his paste and his biscuits and his banana in a nice cool girlie bar with a San Miguel in his hand, the pretty girls on stools, their legs crossed, watching, while he chit-chatted to the Mamasan about prostitution.

'The Japanese are tough, even Chinese too sometimes.'

'Can't be all that tough.' He smiled, he tried to look unconvinced, he was eager for her to give him an example.

'They tie up the girls. They beat them. They treat them badly. For them it is fun but for the girls.' The Mamasan made a face. 'Horrible.'

'They're not afraid of gweilos though.' He was angling again.

'Some of the girls watch porno videos and think all gweilos have big penises like they see. They become afraid that the gweilo will hurt them when he puts it inside.'

'Gweilos like me,' Bunt said.

He hated the Mamasan for smiling at this. 'They know you,' she said. 'They talk.'

'You send these girls to China?'

'No. Girls from the *mah fu*. How you say *mah fu* – someone who takes care of horses, like a horse-trainer?'

'Groom,' Bunt said.

'Yes. They come to me because they owe money to the snake-heads. The girls want more money – to buy a house, start a business.'

The talk of money, of pimps, of snake-heads, of girls

wanting to buy houses and businesses – it all killed his ardor, and made him want to change the subject.

'If I went to China I think they'd kick me out,' he said.

The Mamasan stood up and smiled. 'I kick you in!' and she left him to finish his lunch.

Back in his office he replayed the conversation and his ardor returned. He tried to imagine it, a girl from Hong Kong taking the Kowloon Tong train to China to sleep with a Chinese official. He saw the girl getting off the train, he saw the waiting car, the hotel; then he shook his head, he could not go any further; his imagination failed him. This was a China he did not know.

He felt a flicker of desire, something like thirst in the way his lips were dry, a lightness in his body, like hunger; and his mind slowed, a torpor took over, until he could not think of anything but this simple need. When he was with a woman he seldom had the urge to possess her, he simply talked and laughed, all the while memorizing her, so that afterwards, away from her, with time to reflect, he was stimulated. Distance created desire, nearness made him shy. He was not thinking of the Mamasan and the girls in the Pussy Cat now. He saw Mei-ping, and he wanted her. Her sorrow, the way she had tried to console him, the sadness making her face frail and pretty, the intimation of weakness as she had bowed slightly – she must have been crying, her eyes were swollen – made him desire her all the more.

At the close of work, just before Mr Woo sounded the bell, Bunt found an excuse to be at the exit of the stitching floor. He waited for the bell and then watched the girls gathering their umbrellas and their bags and preparing to leave. Mei-ping looked up at him. He nodded at her.

She did not approach him. She passed him and said, 'Do you want me?'

Her English was poor. Did she know what she was saying?

It aroused him, just hearing that. Of course it was a factory question, everyone said it – Miss Liu said it, Mr Cheung, Mr Woo, everyone, and it was ambiguous – but from Mei-ping's lips it meant one thing.

Mei-ping left with the others. He dismissed Mr Woo. 'Just take the flag down. I'll lock up.' He sat in his office with the door open so that he could watch the elevator, the way it was summoned and descended, the G lighting up and then all the numbers to eight, where he waited, with the blinds drawn, touching his thinning hair with his fingertips.

Not a word. While he locked the door Mei-ping went to his office sofa and sat as she always did, hitched forward, like someone sitting in a bus drawing near their stop, preparing to leave. Bunt went to her and eased her backwards and kissed her. Then he plucked off her blouse – made downstairs, he recognized the label, the cloth, the cut. Soon Mei-ping was kneeling before him while he sat with his mouth open, his head throbbing, his eyes hot. He was panicky but he was caught, and he was afraid, because he was entirely in the spell of this simple young woman. What kept him from blind breathless terror was that she mistook his fear for something else – confidence, perhaps, because he was a man, because he owned the place. Soon he was squawking and snatching at her head.

He made for the Cricket Club afterwards, glad of a place to go, glad of an excuse. He was not ready for Albion Cottage, for his mother, for home, and so the meeting with Monty was welcome. The encounter with Mei-ping had relaxed him and cleared his mind and given him an appetite. The sex had given him a thirst for a beer and a craving for a bacon sandwich.

Bunt did not play cricket, hardly kept track of the scores. He was a member of the Cricket Club for the bowling and the old buffers, the old-timers, his father's friends. He had few friends of his own. As for bowls, though he was absent-minded and too easily distracted to be well coordinated, he could be aggressive and concentrated on the bowling green and was regarded as one of the better players in the club.

Entering the bar – a dreamy smile on his face, he felt lucky, Mei-ping had made it so easy for him – he saw Monty standing at the bar with a Chinese man. Monty imagined that the smile was for him, and was confused when, calling out 'Over here, squire!', Bunt became serious, saying hello. For Bunt the memory was sometimes better than the moment, and Monty had interrupted his reverie.

'Neville, I want you to meet one of our new members.' Monty's hand was on Bunt's neck. 'Mr Hung, Neville Mullard.'

'Pleased to meet you.'

'The pleasure is mine,' the Chinese man said, a bit too explosively.

Bunt said nothing more. He resented the intrusion of this man, for the image of Mei-ping kneeling in his office was quickly fading from his mind.

'I'm buying,' Monty said. 'What's yours, squire?'

'Pint of brain damage.'

'Right you are,' and Monty turned to the bartender.

Mr Hung said, 'You are the owner of the Kowloon Tong Building.'

This was Chinese subtlety: hello and then this big brick hitting the conversation with a thud.

'Imperial Stitching,' Bunt said. 'We used to make all sorts of men's shirts. We do some garments but mostly it's labels. Badges. Name tapes. Fancy stitching. Badges are in demand now. We're reconfiguring them for the Hand-over.' Mr Hung was leaning towards him. 'How do you know I own the building?'

'It is a matter of public record,' Mr Hung said.

It irritated Bunt that Mr Hung spoke English well. The fluent English-speakers in Hong Kong were always the most slippery. They were the least trustworthy, they never meant what they said. Effusive, insincere, mocking; and their good English meant that they had been educated elsewhere, out of the colony, where they had become contemptuous and superior. The ones with American accents were the worst. Bunt liked the locals and their goofy speech – graduates of Hong Kong schools seldom spoke English well, and as a result it kept the class system intact.

'I would like to discuss the purchase of your building,' Mr Hung said.

Bunt laughed out loud at the silliness of it, the way he had just blurted it out. More Chinese finesse!

Mr Hung flinched at the loud laughter that had a tinge of anger – Bunt was still feeling cross at not being able to linger over his memory of Mei-ping. The Chinese man did not take his eyes off Bunt, as though trying to subdue him with his gaze.

Then Monty was putting the drinks down and saying 'squire', and Bunt was smiling again.

'It's not for sale,' Bunt said. He could not resist saying it in a teasing tone. 'I'll never sell it. Don't even think about it – you'll just make yourself miserable.'

FOUR

When he was late and his mother stood waiting in the doorway she always seemed to swell, filling the door frame, to obstruct and delay him, so that she could bulk against his approaching face and scold him. She did it tonight, she had the pathetic aggression of a wife or a mother – to Bunt there was no difference. And sometimes reading tabloid stories about men who committed horrific crimes, he realized that most of those homicidal psychopaths had his precise sort of domestic arrangement: *Middle-aged, soft-spoken, regular in his habits, never married, no friends, sometimes seen leaving strip clubs, lived with his mother, to whom he was devoted.* He hated those stories.

'It's gone eight!' she said, 'I haven't been able to do a thing. Wherever have you been, Bunt?'

Nor did she move from the doorway, and she repeated it to Bunt who could not gain entry.

The question merely bored him. It was not unusual for mother and son to yell at each other. What made him uneasy was the reminder that their lives were synchronized – that they ate and bathed and went to bed and got up at the same time. He liked being punctual, and did not mind seeming predictable, but this was confining and dull. You are forty-three and your mother is nearing seventy and she is telling you that she can't eat because you're not also at the table, and she is repeatedly demanding where were you?

'Doing the accounts,' he said.

He did not look her in the eye – meeting her gaze would have undone him, yet how could he tell her the truth?

'All this Chuck business put me behind. I've been flat out all day.'

His lie immediately helped, as he suspected it would. His mother stepped aside, letting him pass, and she patted his cheek in a sympathetic way. As she lost her anger Bunt felt a jolt of energy, the physical thrill of having kept his secret from her. It was necessary. He knew he was weak, and so any secret made him stronger. Had his mother known how he spent his days his life would have been unbearable. And his stratagem was deeper than merely concealing it from her. Keeping her in the dark was also a way of not having to face the secret himself.

They ate in the lounge, Wang waiting on them.

'I saw Wang jogging today.'

Betty's habit of speaking about Wang as though he were not in the room was her way of making him insecure. She could sense Wang stiffening now, his chin rising, the almost perceptible contraction of his bum cheeks.

His usual jogging route was down the Peak footpath to Wellington, then up again. When people asked Bunt whether he exercised he usually said, 'No, my house-boy does it for me.'

Betty said, 'He looked very impressive in his combinations.'

'Leave off, Mum,' Bunt said. He wanted a bit of peace, his mind was in turmoil.

Just after Mei-ping had left his office he had felt pleasantly drowsy, with a sharpened appetite. Sex in the late afternoon made him anxious but left him in such a stupor of fatigue that he could do nothing about it. The act of sex was for him first a stunning relief, sudden as a sneeze, and an instant

43

later it was the opposite, a sense of helpless suffocation. Once he had seen a Chinese acrobat in the Rainbow Theater at Tsim Sha Tsui balancing his partner on his head – her headstand on his skull – and on each of her upright ankles clusters of gyrating hoops. That had been a thrill for him, because it seemed so dangerous, and when – as he dreaded – the woman faltered and fell, dropping the hoops, Bunt felt it was a metaphor for sex. Sex was a balancing act that always ended in failure, a fall, a sense of having slipped and been inattentive; of not knowing how to explain it. You refused to remember it, and when you tried again the failure was repeated.

And there was the partner to consider: now, that woman knew a secret. It was not as though he had done something wrong alone. It was a conspiracy, but it was unequal. With the onset of desire he found himself pleading and promising. Afterwards, he was empty, with no memory of his lust but only an odd fishy smell on his fingers and a fleeting image of the ridiculous posture he had contrived, the amateur acrobatics, the thrashing legs, even the hoops – no wonder it never worked – he felt tricked and resentful. It was all her fault. And it seemed motiveless as well, because most of them hated it and only did it because he was big needy gweilo.

Bunt had seen them gag and make faces too many times for him to imagine he was giving a woman pleasure. Before they parted, while the woman was still rumpled, her hair askew, her face rubbed and pink, her eyes glazed, he would think, *She looks stuffed*, and wondered whether he looked the same. Sex was their favor to him, who did them many favors. Usually they said, 'You done?' And always, after sex, he hated himself for wanting to say, 'Sorry.'

It was wrong to keep an appointment afterwards, like that one with Monty. He would have preferred a quiet pint of beer and a plate of chips in a darkened club, a little time to resume a calmer identity; an interval, like deliciously smoking a crafty fag between the acts. But the encounter at the Cricket Club, silly and meaningless at the time, had begun to antagonize him. Perhaps it was the presence of Wang, hovering here: Wang somewhat resembled that other man, Hung.

I would like to discuss the purchase of your building was presumptuous and offensive. It was not a building, it was a business; it had products and employees. It was a large busy place, a living thing, and it made a profit. So 'building' rather missed the point.

Bunt was not used to probing questions from strangers, and this stranger Hung was more foreign than most people he had met in Hong Kong, the local strangers. He had looked Bunt in the eye, as Singaporeans did; but his English was far better than that of any Hong Kong or Singapore Chinese, and from its precision and over-correctness Bunt concluded that the man was from China. He had gone to a good school. He had been force-fed the English language in the brainwashing way of Chinese education, and he had learned it for a purpose, which was to con and cheat English-speaking people.

All through dinner Bunt was disturbed. He could not tell his mother about Mei-ping. As for Hung's request, how could he tell his mother if he did not understand it himself?

He had managed to change her tone from scolding to pity. 'Where have you been?' she had said repeatedly to him long ago, when they had lived in Bowen Road, and he had dawdled in the back alleys around Hollywood Road, looking in the rear windows of shops and rooms, hoping to see women in their underwear. In those days he would claim he had a fever, or say 'I hurt my foot,' and she would melt and become motherly and lose all interest in scolding.

He felt so stifled, so possessed by her, that he became childishly insistent on deceiving her in any way he could. His mother knew so much about his life that he deliberately contrived to create secrets – the bar girls, the affairs with employees, Baby the Filipino girl on all fours ('Let we make some fuppies'), and now Mei-ping. The deception was as important as the sex. He needed some room in his life, some space to which she was not admitted. So often he had lived in the space the lie had made for him. There was no truthful way that she would have allowed him this elbow-room. And the lie did not make him feel guilty, but rather the opposite, triumphantly cock-a-hoop, because he had something of his own, no matter how small – it was entirely his secret. That was just one of the satisfactions of a lie. There were others – mastering the trick of deceit, manipulating his mother's mood; lying was story-telling, ventriloquism, mimicry; it made him free.

What made it especially uncomplicated for him to lie to his mother was his assurance that she had never been consistently truthful with him. He often reminded himself that she had taught him to lie – fibbing, she called it; telling whoppers. But he was grateful to her. It was such a consolation to him to have secrets.

She was sorry for him now, sorry for all his work ('I've been flat out'), and he was pleased that he had fooled her so thoroughly and put her in the wrong. He liked it when she was made to feel a bit of remorse; it was right that she, who had put him through so much, should endure a little spell of harmless suffering.

What a waste it would have been to tell her everything. He would only be disgusting her or shaming himself by telling her about Mei-ping. 'You filthy beast,' she would have said. Yet what would her reaction have been to the impertinent offer of that Chinese man to buy the factory?

Had he been able to guess it he might have braved the discussion. *It's their way, isn't it? Chinky-Chonks get their meddling fingers into everything, don't they?*

'You're awfully quiet,' she said.

All this time over dinner he had said nothing.

'All right?' she said.

At times like these, when he was so sunk in his secrets, she had a matron's way of questioning him.

'I'm fine, Mum. Just tired.'

'Course you are. Factory all right?'

'Busy – so many muddles.'

No muddles at all! He had sat watching Mei-ping's pretty hair. He could not recall whether they had kissed. He was not happy being touched, but in this case he was reckless. It was as though she had performed first aid on him, Boy Scout Handbook emergency method for snake-bite. Before she had come to his office he had felt ill, irregular heart-beat, tremulous hands, hot sticky palms, dry mouth. Then she had cured him. She had sucked out the venom from his throbbing wound.

'I hate it when you work late, Bunt.'

'Someone's got to do it.'

Ha! Lunch at the Pussy Cat, sex in his office with the blinds drawn, a pint of brain damage at the Cricket Club with Monty, the pushy Chinese Hung with his probing questions. The sex and the beer had given Bunt a weary overworked look.

Wang was back in the room again, clearing the plates, and Bunt saw Hung in him. It had given him a sense of power to say no to the man – more than a simple no, he had jeered at him. He would never have been able to do that before Mr Chuck died – he would have had to go to the old man's house to repeat the question, seeking his permission to say no, knowing in advance that Mr Chuck, who hated the People's Republic, would never have said yes. Perhaps it was not only the People's Republic that Mr Chuck hated, but rather the Chinese, all of them.

In addition to his excellent English, what was also disconcerting about Mr Hung was his manner. Bunt liked to think that the Chinese were predictable. Bunt could understand them because he understood Mr Chuck and Wang. It bothered him to think that these two men might not be typical, that they might be unlike any other Chinese. It would be so inconvenient. Certainly Mr Chuck's will was an indication of something. Bunt never would have thought the old man wanted him as his heir. He felt he understood Mr Chuck completely, but what about the rest of them?

'Nice bit of beef,' his mother was saying.

Over tea she was reminiscing about the meal they had just eaten.

'Smashing,' Bunt said.

'The sprouts were fresh. From the New Territories. Wang got them today at the market.'

Bunt sipped his tea. Yes, he thought, it was as though Mei-ping had given him first aid for snake-bite, as though a creature had left fang marks and poison in his goolies.

'And I saved you some dripping for breakfast.'

'Ta.'

'The news will be on the wireless. It's five and twenty past nine.'

'Don't, Mum. You know what it's going to be.'

They both knew – the Hand-over. It was the only topic and it was torture, because what could you do about it? Long ago they had reconciled themselves to it. It only confused them to hear more.

His mother said nothing; she watched him as always, with a pained smile, having shifted her teeth in her mouth which gave her an odd bulldog-like grimace and a smile-like bite.

But her expression said nothing. Her mind was crowded with sharp regrets and old sorrows.

Bunt dozed, and on his eyelids were images of Mei-ping's head, her narrow shoulders between his knees, of the Mama-san saying 'horse-trainer,' and 'anything.' And that other disturbing thing, the shocking item in the paper, *Your face belongs to me*. Then he was asleep in his chair, his hand on his head, his head on a purple knitted antimacassar.

At ten-thirty his mother tapped his arm and said, 'Bunt, off you go then.' He woke and yawned and scowled in the lamplight and they each stumbled to their separate rooms, mother and son muttering, ''Night.'

The following day he was on the stitching floor, doing his rounds, when Miss Liu's voice came over the loudspeaker: *Mr Mullard, wanted on Line One.*

His name pronounced by a Chinese person sounded unfamiliar and Irish, and he disliked that. It made him reluctant to go to the phone.

And he also thought, without being able to account for its occurrence just then, that he would never marry anyone to whom he was sexually attracted. He chose women for sex because they were unsuitable for marriage. He had only had sex once with a woman who was neither Chinese nor Filipino and she was a tart in Macao. He thought of the Portuguese as borderline. She told him her name was Rosa Coelho, a common name which he discovered – feeling pity – meant rabbit. Rosa Rabbit was hairy and when she was naked she gave off a shipboard odor of salt and grease. But that was Macao, over the horizon, and did not count. Why was all this coursing restlessly through his head as he approached the telephone on the stitching floor? He did not know.

'Bunt, just a word –'

'Mum?'

'Dinner tonight at Fatty's,' she said.

Fatty's Chop-house in Causeway Bay was his mother's favorite restaurant: spit and sawdust, horse brasses and football pennants, fake beams, a row of pewter tankards on hooks, oak tables, and in the summer 'serving wenches,' so the advertising said. They were most of them illegal immigrants, Vietnamese women who had arrived in Hong Kong as boat people.

'There's someone I want you to meet,' she said.

Long ago, at Fatty's, Bunt had said, 'I imagine London to be full of places like this, except with better food and no Chinese waiters,' and his mother had laughed and said, 'There's a few like it in London but the food's worse and all the waiters are Chinky-Chonks.' She often told the story.

Bunt arrived early but even so his mother was already at the table.

'He let me choose it,' she said, and smiled at her companion.

It was Mr Hung in a new suit with the label sewn to the cuff of his sleeve in an ostentatious way thought by the mainland Chinese to be the height of fashion.

Mr Hung? Bunt smiled insincerely and felt discouraged. The sight of Mr Hung was bad enough, but just as bad was the sight of his mother dressed up. Her formal clothes – stiff-beaded, ill-fitting – were cheap and made her look vulgar. Her plain clothes were sturdy and well made and made her seem sensible. Tonight she looked like a Mamasan.

'My son, Neville.'

'And you are?' Bunt said.

He made a point of not shaking the man's hand, and decided not to acknowledge that he had met the man before. He had kept it from his mother yesterday. Anyway, apparently Mr Hung did not want to let on either.

'My name is Hung, Mr Mullard,' he said. Even though fluent in English, here was another Chinese person giving him an Irish name.

Although Bunt was relieved that Mr Hung was going along with the simple deception of never having met before it made him trust the man even less.

'Mr Hung wanted to go to a Chinese restaurant,' his mother said. 'I had to tell him "Not a chance – I don't eat that muck."'

As Mr Hung fixed his lips in a smile his eyes retreated into his head and his face went unreadable.

'It's adulterated, you know.'

Mr Hung smiled more broadly. Bunt wanted to believe that the man was silent because he did not know the word.

'And I twigged you might be happier here.'

That meant that she did not want him to see her as selfish for choosing Fatty's for herself, which was exactly what she had done.

'Bunt loves a bit of beef,' she said. 'We're beef eaters – very English in that respect. But they have all sorts here. Steaks and chops, and they do a lovely sausage and pud. Proper toad-in-the-hole. English-type bangers, with bread. None of your continental kind.'

Mr Hung was still smiling and tapping a Fatty's Chop-house match cover through his fingers.

'I have to laugh,' Betty said, and laughed, and began to tell the story of the time Bunt had said, 'I imagine London to be full of places like this.'

'Mum,' Bunt said, and she stopped.

But a moment later, winking at Bunt, she started to tell the story of the time at the beach on Silver Mine Bay, one Sunday while George was still alive, and Bunt had farted –

'Mum,' Bunt said, stopping her again.

The punch-line of that story was Bunt turning to look at his own bum and saying, 'Quiet, botty!'

From his fixed smile and his silence and his nervous finger-tapping, it was clear that Mr Hung had not the slightest idea of what the woman was saying. Bunt could tell that, however good the man's ear for English might be, it did not extend to peculiarities such as food, or his mother's south London accent, or her mumbling drawl caused by her loose dentures. Those childhood stories were dreadful, but he liked his mother better for her being a challenge to Hung's English.

'Here I am chin-wagging and I fancy you want your beer, Mr Hung. I know Bunt wants his beer.'

'I will have a cup,' Mr Hung said.

'Of tea?'

'Of beer,' Mr Hung said.

That was very Chinese, his getting his containers muddled.

'A cup of beer for Mr Hung,' Bunt said, to mock him.

There was a stack of presents beside Betty's place-mat: a bottle of red wine, a box of chocolates, a leather coin purse, a flower sealed in clear plastic. Bunt did not ask about them; he knew the answer.

Betty had a shandy, Bunt guzzled his beer, Mr Hung sipped but did not drink. They ordered their meal, Betty tried to tell another story ('We're on a tram and Bunt looks up and says, "Mum, why has that man got his mouf open?"'), but Bunt stopped her again. The food was served and, this being Fatty's, it was piled on trenchers and pewter platters. Now, eating, no one spoke for a minute or more.

'Lovely bit of beef,' Betty said.

Mr Hung cleared his throat and said, 'Will you tell him, please?'

Bunt smirked at the man's lack of subtlety, but he was

grateful, too. He would be just as forthright in his reply as the presumptuous man had been in his question.

Betty chewed her meat and with her mouth full she said, 'Mr Hung has got a proposition for us.'

Bunt was still trying to suppress his smirk, knowing what was coming.

Swallowing her meat and dabbing at the blood on her lips, she went on, 'He wants to buy the factory.'

'And I hope you told him we're not interested in his proposition.'

Now his mother was smiling. She said, 'Hang on, that's not the proposition, is it?'

Mr Hung beamed, seeming to approve of the way the mother was sparring with the son, like an old lioness swinging her broad paw and batting an unruly cub, pleased that her effort was on his behalf.

'Bunt, what do you reckon that old factory is worth?'

'If by "old factory" you mean Imperial Stitching, I haven't a clue,' he said. He was thoroughly disgusted. How had Hung found her? Bunt added, 'A packet, no question. But it's not a factory. It's a business. We have many employees, we make things, we earn a substantial profit. It is more than a livelihood – it is a living thing.'

'Four or five million?'

'I wouldn't be surprised.'

But truly he had no idea, and these sums did surprise him. He had never thought of Imperial Stitching in dollars or pounds. It was his life, and a life had no money value. They had always had a half share in Imperial. It had hardly sunk in that they now owned Mr Chuck's half as well.

'He's offering us seven-plus,' Betty said. 'Top whack. A million quid.'

Bunt had resumed eating, so as to seem uninterested, and he was beginning to choke from the effort of it. How he hated holding this conversation about the factory and money in the presence of this intrusive Chinese man who was a perfect stranger. His mother saying *A million quid* made him cringe, in just the same way he had cringed when his father used an obscenity.

'And you think that's an attractive proposition?' Bunt said at last.

Betty glanced at Mr Hung who was gloating at her, as though urging her to defy her son.

'That's the price,' his mother said. She had shoved her chair back and was getting to her feet. 'That's not the proposition. You tell him, Mr Hung, while I spend a penny.'

Mr Hung smiled at her. 'When I am through,' he said, 'you will be able to spend more than a penny.'

Bunt was squinting. He said, 'Pardon?'

FIVE

'You made it plain as day you didn't want to know. But why bite his nose off like that?'

As she spoke, Betty interrupted herself by puffing out her downy cheeks and blowing on her cup of Milo. They were back home at Albion Cottage on the fog-smothered Peak, having one of Wang's hot drinks before taking turns in the bathroom and removing their pajamas from the airing-cupboard (each had a shelf) – more night-time rituals that Bunt found more unsettling on days he spent with Baby or Mei-ping. Not that he felt dissolute or sinful, simply unfaithful, as though he was neglecting his mother. When a woman was tearing off his jumper he sometimes reflected: *My mother knitted this jumper*.

Bunt said, 'I wasn't interested in his proposition.'

'If only you'd listened a titch more.'

'I heard what I wanted to.'

At times like this he was reminded uncomfortably of sounding like his father, and even felt like a little old man being henpecked by a bossy wife. He loved his mother, and sometimes sorrowed for her lack of education – the poor woman had not gone past form four; yet he needed to be selfish so as not to be overwhelmed by his pity for her in her early bereavements – the loss of Bunt the First, and her ignorant and suffocating attention. He sometimes sensed that her bullying warnings about local women, all of them self-serving, had made him over-eager and reckless. That had apparently been the case with his father, if the Mamasan could be believed.

'It sounded jolly interesting to me.'

Betty took a gulp of Milo and worked it around her dentures, with her lips pressed shut, not swallowing it, but sloshing it like mouthwash.

'All that money,' she said.

'There'll be more down the road.'

'Wrong end of the stick there, Bunt,' his mother said. 'The future of the colony is nebulous.'

Bunt smiled at this perfect word of precise polysyllables on his mother's damp lips. 'The Hand-over, Mum. That's pretty certain.'

'But after the Chinese Take-away it's all a muddle,' she said. 'Funnily enough, when our friend Mr Hung explained his proposition to me I was bored rigid. Then the penny dropped. It's as though he's doing us a favor.'

'Some favor.'

'Ready money, Bunt.'

'The company's flush.'

'The factory's a pup.'

She called it the factory, the works, the godown; he called it the company or simply Imperial. It was eight floors, three of them occupied by workers on machines, an office floor – Executive Offices, one floor of machines covered in dust sheets, a storage floor, Shipping, Dispatch.

'It's entirely ours. Mr Chuck made sure of that. Doesn't that mean something?'

'All the other stitching beavered off to China. How can we compete with China?'

'This will be China next year.'

'Queen Anne's dead,' his mother sighed. 'Don't be such a binder, Bunt.'

But he was gesturing for her to let him finish. 'And then we can compete.'

'They'll issue us with ID cards.'

'We've got ID cards now, Mum.'

'These tatty little learner permits are not IDs. I am talking about ID cards that say Big Brother is Watching You.'

'What does it matter what it says when we've also got British passports?'

'A UK passport is a license to eff off. They could ban them. They could make us take Chinky-Chonk nationality.' She sloshed a mouthful of Milo. 'Which makes sense. As you said, Hong Kong will be China.'

'Are you saying you'd get a Chinese passport?'

'Not on your nelly.' She was sloshing once more and he thought she might spit, for she was glancing around as though for a spittoon, but instead she swallowed.

'So we sell to Mr Hung,' Bunt said. 'Then what?'

'We'll go back to UK and find a suitable location. Something on the coast. A chalet bungalow. Freehold. Newish.'

He felt married to her again.

'It's cold and awful there.'

'Cheap and cheerful,' she said. 'And we'll have – what – a million quid.'

'Million' in his mother's mouth was a meaningless word. She seemed foolish the moment she uttered it. Bunt could almost imagine having a million pounds, but he could not imagine spending a million. Whatever would you spend it on? There was nothing, apart from another badge manufacturer, that he would want to own, or that would consume a million pounds. Even if they bought a new house, a new car, a new TV, central heating, smoked salmon, and all the other luxuries that people bought, there would still be hundreds of thousands left, and what for?

'We don't need ready money,' Bunt said. 'Our bills are paid. We're better off with a company like Imperial.'

'In Hong Kong?'

'Of course.'

'Gweilos have no future here, Bunt,' his mother said. 'That's why I say, "Take the million."'

Take the million! To Bunt there was something hilarious in his mother's again casually mentioning a million – she who would often risk being hit by a scooter as she delved into dustbins for used tram tickets, who soaked unfranked stamps and peeled them from envelopes to use again – used the old envelopes too; licked the lids of jam jars, used the jam jars for tumblers; saved string as assiduously as her late husband, from whom she had learned the habit; rinsed and saved old sauce bottles, kept her old flannel underwear in the rag basket – it still seemed strange to Bunt when he saw Wang dusting the lounge with his mother's knickers. Her mention of a million made her seem credulous and clownish.

For one thing, anyone who used the word 'quid' had never had a million of anything, and certainly not pounds sterling. When she said 'million' you were reminded more strongly than ever that she was plain Betty Mullard of Balham, who had still not lived down a note she had scribbled to George after the coal man had delivered his load, saying, *Colemans bin.*

'Use your bonce,' she said.

'I didn't like the sound of his scheme.'

'He had thought it all out.'

'It sounded dodgy.'

'You were looking at him squiffy-eyed.'

'Because he's a nasty piece of work.'

'How do you know that? You'd never clapped eyes on him before.'

It was not too late to reveal to her that he had and that the encounter at Monty's instigation had not been a success.

'He's nicely spoken,' his mother said.

He thought: Trust her, so common herself, to be a snob about accents. Yet it was in character and as English as her home-made cardigan and the way her clicking dentures made her whistle, for it was a shop assistant's way of mocking – the self-inflicted snobbery of sneering at people just like herself, on behalf of her equally snobbish customers.

His mother's opinions reminded Bunt of how his father had met his future bride at the Army & Navy in Victoria Street. Betty had been behind the counter in Fancy Goods. Her mother's family had been nearly destitute and her father's had been 'in service' – her father, a gambler, had been bankrupt: she referred to him with a kind of hauteur as 'a gentleman's gentleman.' He polished silver, laboring with it, using paste. 'He wore white gloves.' But that was futile boasting. She had also once tearfully told her son how the poor man, dogged by gambling debts, had walked the streets of south London trying to work up the courage to kill himself. He had not done himself in, and instead had gone home to Balham, gray-faced with depression, feeling even more like a failure. 'But he was nicely spoken.' The very mention of his accent maddened Bunt and made him want to drop his aitches.

'Mr Hung is not one of our local Chinky-Chonks.'

'Mr Chuck was local, but so what?'

'Mr Chuck was a gentleman,' his mother said.

The Chinese partner had acquired that status since his death.

'And a very generous man,' she said. 'Have another oatie, Bunt.'

'I'm stuffed. Go ahead, Mum.'

'I know when I've had enough,' she said.

So that was it? But no: it concerned him that she said nothing more about the proposition now, because it meant that she had more to say and was saving it for later – tomorrow, next week, all month, until the Take-away. She wanted 'a million quid.' She would try to wear him down in order to get it. She gabbled when she was confused, but when her mind was teeming and fuddled she could not think and she sat in an enigmatic or truculent silence, as though Bunt were to blame for her bewilderment. He was tired. When he was alone with his mother she sucked out his vitality.

And so another evening ended: chinwag, Milo, bathroom, airing-cupboard, bed.

The following day, a Saturday, Mr Hung invited Betty and Bunt to his apartment in central Kowloon. He had something to give them, he said. 'It's on the way to your building.'

Bunt refused, but his mother insisted. 'It's on the way to the factory' – Bunt was stopping at Imperial to pick up the mail. 'And when someone offers you something, you don't fling it back in his face.'

'I'll go alone,' Bunt said. He felt that his mother had already been too compliant; he wanted to show Mr Hung that he was not impressed with the proposition to buy Imperial Stitching.

Bunt could not remember a time when he had been invited to a Chinese apartment in the colony. Hong Kong people met in restaurants; they were secretive about their houses. Was it because a house and its furnishings said too much about you? Or was it the disorder, everyone in pajamas, shuffling in sandals, howling at each other, the noise of the neighbors, the squalor?

Whatever, Bunt had also agreed to go out of curiosity and

for the novelty of the invitation. And Mr Hung was right: the apartment was on the way, a ten-minute walk from Imperial.

Mr Hung welcomed him in his designer suit with the maker's label stitched to the sleeve. It was on the eighth floor of a building near Argyle Street. From one window he could see Hong Kong and the ridge above the Peak tramway where Albion Cottage stood sheltered among some trees; from the opposite window Imperial Stitching was like an old monument on the Kai Tek flight path.

'Tea?'

'Thanks, no. I've got to run. You mentioned you had something for my Mum?'

'And you.'

Bunt was glad when Mr Hung left the room, because he wanted to take a good look at its furnishings. When someone came to Imperial to take out an order, Bunt often sent Mr Woo down to the car park to have a look at the man's car – what make, what year, what condition? You would have a pretty good idea of the person's character – Chinese or British – from the car.

The white shag carpets in Mr Hung's apartment were puzzling, and so was the glass-fronted cabinet with its shelves of blue china bowls and the sort of porcelain Chinese soup spoons that looked like shoe-horns. When Bunt walked towards it on the uneven floor all the china rattled. The clock on the altar-like Chinese sideboard was ridiculous – fake French, standing on claw feet of fake gilt, fake wooden case, absurd ticking. On the glass-topped coffee table there was an ashtray. Beside it was a matchbook cover: *Fatty's Chop-house*. The base of the ashtray read *Golden Dragon*. That was elegant: Hung had pinched an ashtray from a Kowloon restaurant.

To needle Mr Hung, Bunt said, 'Mr Chuck used to eat there.'

'I'm glad you are aware of that,' Mr Hung said. He was not in the least put off by Bunt's needling; indeed, he actually did seem glad that Bunt had pointed this out.

The pilfered items only made the place seem more shoddy and impersonal, but it was like a glimpse into Mr Hung's head, and in order to see more he said, 'May I use the facilities?'

A white shag carpet in there, too. And the lid was down on the WC. One of Mr Mo's *feng-shui* instructions was: 'Keep the WC covered with its seat flap or the *Ch'i* will leave the building by rushing down the hole.'

When he returned to the parlor he saw that Mr Hung had set out the presents. They were Chinese presents, cheap and ill-assorted; these little gifts did not impose a burden of indebtedness, they were merely symbols of generosity in a Chinese ritual of gift-giving.

A basket of fruit, including longans, lychees and mangos – very nice, but Bunt was thinking, 'I could have bought these at the market.' Candied plums, 'and what's this?' Bunt wondered. Mr Hung said, 'A range of cold snacks.' His mother would not touch them with a barge pole. An embroidered kitten, in silk, sealed in a large plastic lozenge. An umbrella. A pair of cushion covers. A thermos flask. 'Deer Horn Embrocation.' 'Lung Ching Tea' in a gaily colored tin caddy with a painted lid. A wooden box, with a hinged lid, containing a bottle of *mao tai* liquor.

Bunt expressed surprise and pleasure at Mr Hung's stubborn habit of meanness, knowing the presents would only irritate his mother. All these inexpensive presents proved to Bunt that Mr Hung was not to be trusted. He took them home that evening in two bags.

Betty said that she would have been more suspicious if

the presents had been expensive. That would have been confusingly out of character.

'Give him a chance,' she said.

'The answer is still no,' Bunt said.

On the Monday, Mr Hung rang Bunt at the factory.

'I was wondering whether you were free this evening for a drink.'

'I don't drink on a Monday at the Cricket Club,' Bunt said.

'I was hoping we might meet at a more lively venue such as the Pussy Cat.'

'Sorry,' Bunt said.

Why had Hung suggested the Pussy Cat?

That same week Mei-ping knocked shyly at his office door after work. She was wearing a loose blue fluffy sweater, cashmere perhaps, that Bunt wanted to touch. She was smiling sweetly.

'Just to thank you,' she said.

Bunt drew back, put his hand into his pocket. What was she talking about?

'For the jumper,' she said.

And Bunt stared, because it was the most expensive item in her wardrobe, and because he had not given it to her.

She laughed shyly as she said, 'The Chinese man said it was your idea. Made in China.' She touched the seams expertly with her fingers, finding the stitches. 'It's good work.'

So Hung had given it to her and in so doing he was informing Bunt that he knew of their arrangement – their meetings after work, the secret drinking, the furtive sex – but just how did he know? It was a dreadful way to send a message, because Bunt could not tell the truth and warn Mei-ping without terrifying her about this interfering sneak.

She stood there in his office door wearing her new sweater, and Bunt became anxious again, realizing that someone knew his secret, and that it was Mr Hung.

'Do you want me?'

'No,' he said. 'Please go.'

'Thanks again,' Mei-ping said, making him miserable. He wanted to embrace her but he felt that Mr Hung was watching him.

Needing a drink, he went that evening to Jack's Place and downed two whiskies. Baby the Filipino girl was there with her friend Luz. Why weren't they where they belonged, at the Pussy Cat?

'We pollow you,' Luz said.

Baby said, 'I think you don't like me any more.'

'I've got a lot on my mind,' Bunt said.

'Nobody be perfect.' *Perpeck*. 'So dance with me, Neville.'

When had he told her his real name? He had always made a point of giving false names, and so the intrusion into his privacy alarmed him. He had two more drinks, and then he was not worried any more. But he was puzzled when, trying to pay for his whiskies, he was told there was no charge.

'Your friend paid,' Luz said.

She laughed and began dancing with Baby. Seeing the two women dancing, Bunt hesitated and watched with fascination. But he was soon panicky again. What friend?

Mr Hung knew his movements, his girlfriends, the bars he frequented. Back at Albion Cottage that night his mother waited, filling the doorway, as she always did when he was late.

'Why are you looking at me like that?'

'Got a cough pastille in my gob, haven't I?'

She worked her teeth sideways and made a face.

'Nice jumper,' he said.

'Present from our friend.'

'Oh Lord,' Bunt said, and felt ill.

'You're ghastly, I knew you would be,' his mother said.
And then, sighing, added, 'Oh, pack it in! I could do business
with that man.'

SIX

On Thursday, his bowling night at the Cricket Club, he decided to bring the matter up with Monty, but to do so obliquely. *I have a friend who is wondering about the Hand-over* ... He had never spoken about the Hand-over – what was the point? Everyone had an opinion, but no one agreed on what the final outcome would be. And nothing could be done. It was like a spell of weather that was forecast and that would soon cover Hong Kong. But this front had no end; it was a permanent change. Hong Kong was getting a new climate.

'Evening, squire.'

Before he could respond, Monty made a beckoning gesture. For a moment, Bunt dreaded that he might be beckoning Mr Hung again, but no: it was an American, oddly dressed in an expensive suit and cowboy boots, a big silver buckle on his belt, a blue shirt, a loud silk tie.

'Neville, I want you to meet Hoyt Maybry, one of my colleagues just visiting from our Singapore office.'

Bunt said hello. Denied a handshake, Hoyt Maybry flexed his fingers.

'Neville runs the family business.'

'And what might that be?'

'Textiles,' Bunt said.

'We've done some successful joint-ventures,' Hoyt said. 'China's made a quantum leap in textiles. I'm talking top of the line product. The biggest labels. They're streaking past Hong Kong.'

Bunt said, 'Because we don't employ children.'

'Hold on,' Hoyt said, because Monty was laughing. 'I want to reply to that.'

'Oh, belt up, I've heard it already,' Bunt said. 'You Yanks!'

Monty said, 'He's teasing you.'

'Hong Kong is an accident of history that is about to be rectified,' Hoyt said.

'Hong Kong was doing perfectly well as a British colony,' Bunt said.

'Sure. No elections. No democracy. The old school tie, old boy network,' Hoyt said. 'Give me a break.'

Bunt said, 'There was freedom here. Granted it was a free-for-all, survival of the fittest, but it worked, and it was better than anything the Chinese will do with all their bloody policemen, or you Americans talking all your sanctimonious balls about democracy.'

'The Chinese are kind of funny,' Hoyt said. 'The way I look at it, they're basically giving you the finger the whole time. That's Chinese philosophy – the finger.'

Monty said, 'There's a lot in what Hoyt is saying.'

Hoyt was smiling at Bunt. He said, 'So how long have you been here?'

'I was born here,' Bunt said, and ignoring the American he turned to Monty. He said, 'A friend of mine has been offered a proposition from a Chinese official. I don't know all the details.'

'Doesn't matter,' Hoyt said. 'Just do quick and dirty figures and build in a big fudge factor.'

'Excuse me?' And Bunt turned back to Monty. 'It goes like this. My friend's property is worth seven million. The proposition is to form a foreign company that constitutes a third party. The purchase price is pegged at nine million.

The Chinese official pays nine million from his ministry's funds. The money is wired to the new company. The seller – this friend of mine gets seven, plus a percentage of the additional money, another million or so.'

Monty was listening calmly, while the American Hoyt had begun to smile.

'Have you ever heard of a deal like that?'

Hoyt said, 'Is there any other kind of deal?'

Bunt was stung – ashamed of his innocence. But at least he had protected himself with this talk of his friend. He had given nothing away.

'There's an awful lot of money around at the moment, tremendous liquidity,' Hoyt said. 'Twenty-five billion is earmarked for China in US and international direct investments.'

'My friend hasn't made up his mind,' Bunt said. He looked squarely at Hoyt. 'He says he's in it for the long haul.'

'The smart money is moving out,' Monty said.

'I want to see what's going to happen,' Bunt said.

'There's a boom coming,' Hoyt said.

'I'll tell you what's going to happen,' Monty said. 'In small insidious ways, the PRC will tighten the noose. Look at the schools, the lessons about the British. You think they're going to be teaching the British view of colonialism? It will be the official Chinese version of world history. Look at immigration. Who will qualify? Only the people the Chinese want. They'll boot out the rest. In business we'll all need work permits – a chit to do business. All these can be revoked.'

'If a person looks a little hinky they'll send him away,' Hoyt said.

'That includes you,' Bunt said, 'and all the other Americans.'

Monty said, 'Hoyt's not American.'

As though reciting a rhyme, for he had clearly said it before, Hoyt explained, 'I am American. I am not *an* American.'

'What does that mean?' Bunt asked.

'I renounced my citizenship.'

'How'd you manage that?'

'Not too hard. Went to the US Consulate. Signed a statement. Went home. Next day went back again, signed an Oath of Renunciation. Handed over my passport.' Hoyt hooked his thumbs into his belt. 'That's how I got rich.'

'I'll never turn my back on the UK,' Bunt said.

Monty said, 'Take the partners in my firm. Kwok's a Canadian. Lum's a Tongan Protected Person. Levine's a Cayman Islander. From where I am sitting in this club I can see Cape Verdeans, Belizeans and Panamanians.'

All this was news to Bunt, who saw Englishmen, most of whom he knew.

'I've got a Guinea-Bissau passport,' Hoyt said.

'Where the hell is that?'

'Not too far from Cape Verde,' Hoyt said. 'So I'm told.'

'One of the fuzzy-wuzzy countries. That makes you a nig-nog.'

'Watch it,' Hoyt said.

'And you're an Israeli, I suppose,' Bunt said to Monty, because he knew him to be Jewish.

'Austrian,' Monty said. He was sipping at the foam on his stein of beer. 'It was the Austrian consul here who proposed it. He came to me. He knew a bit of my family background.' He licked at the froth on his upper lip. He said with seriousness, 'I saw it as an act of atonement on their part.'

'Monty, you're a kraut?'

'Austrians aren't krauts,' Monty said. 'You're thinking of Germans.'

'Isn't it the same place?'

Bunt was shocked, because Monty had always spoken fondly of his father's medical practice in Whitechapel, his devotion to his patients, Monty's own education at LSE and his office in Chancery Lane. A real Londoner, with a bowler hat and a tightly rolled umbrella, that was how he thought of Monty, while he himself was a colonial, with just a public school education at Queen's College in Hong Kong.

'Not at all,' Monty said, raising his beer stein again. 'I'm from a long line of Viennese intellectuals.'

Bunt did not blame him, he blamed Hong Kong, the way it cut off people's roots and made them selfish and sneering and greedy and spineless, even his own mother. He made no reply. He looked around the Cricket Club and realized that they would bolt at the first sign of trouble.

Monty said, 'If your friend wants to do business, tell him to get in touch with me.'

'Or me,' Hoyt said.

Bunt was on the verge of saying *Which friend?* when he remembered.

His mother had a new basket of fruit that night when he returned to Albion Cottage. Why was she so happy? A basket of fruit was a basket of fruit. At his office the next day, Mei-ping brought a basket of fruit to his office. Another one. This was loquats and longans and mangosteens and kiwi fruit. She held it in her pretty hands.

'The man give this to you.'

'Which man?' He opened the note taped to the basket. *Please call.*

'From China I think. I don't know him.'

'But he knows you?'

'Maybe.'

Bunt hated that equivocal *maybe*, which meant that he would have to obey the suggestion in the accompanying note.

Seeing Mei-ping leave his office he was attracted to her again – there was such innocence in the way she and most women walked away, always looking a little helpless and uncertain and awkward. Most men walked swaggeringly away as though at any moment they might turn around and snarl, but women always seemed to be retreating. Bunt often felt like seizing their skinny shoulders and dragging them down, and he hated himself for his demented rapist's fantasies.

When he rang Mr Hung later that morning the man answered at once, snatched up the receiver – must have done – as though he had been hovering near it all week, waiting for its bell to sound.

'*Wei*,' he said, surprised into his mother tongue, and then, 'Yes?'

'There is something I'd like to see you about,' Bunt said, hoping to put him on the defensive.

'Thank you for returning my call,' Mr Hung said, neatly sidestepping. 'I am so glad you received my message.'

'I don't have a great deal of time,' Bunt said.

'I have even less,' Mr Hung said. 'Let's say the club at six.'

'Cricket Club?'

'Pussy Cat,' Mr Hung said, and put the phone down before Bunt could raise an objection.

Bunt could not say why he felt at a disadvantage meeting Mr Hung this way. Yet he did – he felt unprotected. Mr Hung was at his cheeriest and most reasonable. Perhaps that was it, the confidence of the man, the fact that he had already insinuated himself into Bunt's life – was on excellent terms with his mother, knew Mei-ping, the Mamasan, Baby and

Luz, was probably intimate with Monty too; Mr Hung had in this way taken charge.

They met coincidentally by the shrine on the side wall of the club, a devil goddess gloating in a red box, lit by two red bulbs. Mr Hung took no interest, but as always Bunt was mildly alarmed by it. They were shown by the Mamasan to a booth in the back. Mr Hung seemed familiar with the Pussy Cat, he greeted Wendell the barman – who gave him a hearty wave before turning back to the TV set; and that made Bunt uneasy too. No girls came near – that had to have been prearranged by Hung.

Mr Hung said, 'Drink?'

'Nothing for me,' Bunt said. 'I don't want any more presents, so please stop sending them.'

Mr Hung's face was in shadow, but Bunt suspected that the man was smiling grimly when he said, 'I asked you to meet me here precisely because there are no more presents for you.'

Bunt who had rehearsed a denunciation of the gift-giving was caught unprepared and did not know what to say to this.

'Not that they were especially valuable,' Bunt said. 'The fruit was bruised, and oddly enough we do own a thermos flask or two.'

Mr Hung said, 'I think you will wish me to ignore what you have just said,' and in his smiling, sneering way he sounded very sinister. But how could he be a threat, this Chinese stranger?

'Listen,' Bunt said. 'We're very happy with our company and premises. We have no intention of selling.'

'I know that,' Mr Hung said. 'But there are several things you do not know.'

The music in the club was rather loud. It stimulated Bunt to the point where he wondered whether it would do any good to shout at the man, as the singer was shouting now.

'One is that if you do not sell you will not be happy next year.'

'You know that, do you?'

'Yes. I will be in a position to make you unhappy.'

Bunt had been right, Mr Hung had come here attempting to threaten him, and he trembled with anger at the arrogance of the Chinese intruder.

'I don't have to listen to this, mate.'

'But you would be wise to listen.'

'Uttering menaces is a crime under English law. I could have a constable over here from Lai Chi Kok, and you'd be in stir.'

'I don't think so. After all, we're in a club where you are well known for drunkenness and much more. Would you want that to become known?'

'You're trying to threaten me.'

'Not at all,' Mr Hung said. 'After the thirtieth of June next near I will be in Hong Kong in an official capacity, which is the acquisition of strategic sites for the People's Liberation Army. Next year it will not be a suggestion, but a command, an order which you will obey.'

The mocking music played loudly and now there were people dancing, the prostitutes and the gweilos, Baby, Luz, the others.

'I'll take my chances,' Bunt said.

'The price will be much less. We will provide our own assessment of the value of your site.'

'See if I care.'

'The sale will be enforced by military decree. The price will be fixed. And we might decide to pay you in renminbi. You will be able to spend it in China but nowhere else.'

Bunt said, 'You *are* threatening me.'

'I am telling your fortune,' Mr Hung said.

That stopped Bunt cold. Now he wished, twisting his hands, that he had a drink.

'If you don't accept a substantial profit now in hard currency, you will receive less next year in yuan. Either way you will sell, willingly now, or next year under pressure. It is not a choice. It is merely a matter of time. The rice is cooked.'

'I think you're bluffing. How do I know you're a high official?'

'Instead of asking whether you know me, consider how much I know about you,' Mr Hung said. 'I know of your relationship with Mei-ping and the Filipino girl. Wendell is a so-called Eurasian.'

'What's that got to do with anything?'

Hung said, 'I am showing you that I am well acquainted. I also know that you have a separate bank account that even your mother is not aware of. I know the balance in it. I know that you have mislabeled some of your goods –'

'Everyone does that,' Bunt said, hoping to stop him.

'And you have kept the proceeds, which means an irregularity on your tax returns. British tax returns, of course. But next year they will be Chinese tax returns. In China embezzling is a crime against the people. Embezzlers are given a short trial and then shot in the back of the head. Shall I go on?'

'Don't bother.'

'Next year you will be begging to sell.'

Mr Hung had almost convinced him. Bunt was terrified by what the man knew.

Bunt said, 'Next year you won't make a profit.'

'Neither will you,' Mr Hung said. 'Do you see why it is so necessary that we become partners?'

'I don't want to be your partner. I don't like you. In fact, I hate you,' Bunt said. 'You're a spotty bottom.'

Now Bunt was certain that Mr Hung was smiling. 'That is irrelevant,' he said. 'You probably don't like your employees either. But they do their work, so you pay them.'

It was what Bunt had often felt, it was something his mother had said out loud; how did Mr Hung know it?

'A woman you have sex with is one that you need, not one that you love,' Mr Hung said.

Again it was like a glimpse into his heart, and he was ashamed and fearful.

'I am telling you that you need me,' Mr Hung said.

'You need me too!'

Mr Hung jerked his head sideways at Bunt's shout, and his face caught a bit of light from the dance floor. His smile, the worst feature of his face, rattled Bunt badly.

'Think of yourself.'

It was what everyone said. But this man was different. For the first time Bunt was hearing this solemn truth from a Chinese person, a man who claimed to be a government official.

'You have no future here.'

Bunt was not wholly convinced. But something else took hold of him, the certainty that next year and in the future there would be more men like this – smiling, pestering, threatening, insinuating; and enforcing the law, all the new clauses about subversion and disloyalty. This was the future of Hong Kong, a Chinese system of threats and bribes and crookery, whispers of dire consequences in disreputable places like this, and it would be like the old system, except that he would not be a UK citizen any more in a British colony, he would be a UK citizen in a Chinese Special Administrative Region, he would be the ultimate gweilo.

Bunt stared across the table in this shadowy booth. In the uncertain light of the Pussy Cat Hung's face had the malign expression of the devil goddess in the red box by the door, the Mamasan's shrine, with a bright fruit in a bowl as an offering. Next year there would be more diabolical men like Mr Hung, and he knew he would hate them all. He would want out.

He said, 'I'll have to ask my mother.'

'Your mother has already agreed to the terms.'

Hung was right about her, too.

Bunt hurried out of the Pussy Cat. He would not have minded being seen with a prostitute, but he did not want to be seen leaving with Mr Hung.

Monty did not seem surprised when Bunt told him of his decision. They used the conference room of Brittain, Kwok, Lum and Levine in Hutchison House. A holding company was formed in the Cayman Islands. They called it Full Moon, because on the day of its formation the moon was full over Kowloon Tong. The price of Imperial Stitching was fixed at nine million Hong Kong dollars, seven million for the site, two million to split evenly between Mr Hung and the Mullards, mother and son.

'The total ticket will be eight, squire.'

Bunt said, 'Just don't tell the employees.'

SEVEN

As soon as he had agreed to the sale to Mr Hung of Imperial Stitching Bunt felt miserable and regretted it. The money was huge but the money did not really matter, and even the word 'million' was no consolation. His mind was unsettled by the thought of Mr Hung's bony face and crooked smile, and he kept seeing him as he saw him in the booth, with a sinister shadow across his eyes, like the vindictive squint of a Chinese idol. This one could not be propitiated with a ripe orange or a cluster of smoldering joss sticks. His message was, *Do as I say or you're finished*. So it was not the money, it was the threat.

Bunt told himself over and over, *I had no choice*.

It was as though, even before any negotiation, Hung regarded himself as owner of the factory, and would not consider any alternative; that Bunt had to face the fact that he would have to hand it over. But the idea that Mr Hung was forcing him to do it began to rankle.

Unexpectedly, his mother's happiness made him more miserable. It was not just the money, 'a million quid,' it was also that in selling it she had managed to take long overdue revenge upon her husband, whom Bunt now realized she had hated. He keenly recalled her saying, 'But I do apportion blame.'

She was suspicious and over-protective towards Bunt because he was so much like his father. Now Bunt understood his father's life, his mother's resentment. She could not forgive George his dalliance with his Chinese workers or his indiscretions with the Filipino bar hostesses; the sneaking into 'chicken houses' and 'phoenix rooms,' the massage parlors, the blue hotels, the lame explanations. And what did she know of the Mamasan?

'He made a fool of me,' Betty said.

The prospect of ready money emboldened her and made her vengeful. She had never comprehended credit, or interest payments, or paper profits, or even a bank book stamped with numbers; but the notion of a brick of rose-colored Hong Kong and Shanghai Bank notes, secured with brown tape, in her handbag, three inches of cash smelling of fresh ink, gave her a sense of power and something like health. *That's what I need, Bunt, a bit of encouragement from the Honkers and Shankers.*

'He had an eye for the ladies, that one,' she said. 'Always out on the tiles.'

Bunt was silent, cringing inwardly: talking that way about his father she was also talking about him.

The deal with Mr Hung had been eagerly struck on her part. No threat had been needed to persuade her – she had been surprised and grateful, and yet this creepy Chinese man from the mainland with his good command of English still worried Bunt. For Bunt, Hung was a scarecrow. His mother had been greatly motivated in the deal by revenge against her husband, though she always protested that she loved her husband; and by the money – she who had no use for money.

It was always the poor who had the most unrealistic notions of money. Bar girls were capable of making insane demands, when they made demands. 'I need ten thousand,' Baby had said to him once, and he had just laughed. She believed she had power over him, that her sexual virtuosity had bewitched him. It arose from 'Let we make some fuppies.'

78

Each time he requested it, she would hesitate and say, 'When you take me to England we do it all the time.' Once, as though to tempt him, she had shown up at the Pussy Cat wearing a leather dog-collar around her neck. That would be his reward for her doggy tricks: in return for her bending over he would look after her, and her mother, and her sister, and perhaps others, for the rest of their lives. But he was not a slave to sex. The act was brief and all he wanted afterwards was to be alone with a pint of beer and a plate of greasy chips or a bacon sandwich.

When a hard-up person named a figure it was always absurd – sometimes a pittance, more often a fortune. And they were just as silly in talking about houses or cars. 'Why you don't have a Mercedes Benz?' Luz asked him one rainy night – he was giving her a lift – jeering at his Rover. Luz was from Manila, city of bangers and jitneys. They were single-minded, and credulous, and you could never please them, and that was why a million was meaningless, just funny money.

He suspected that of Mr Hung, a Chinese man who could not possibly ever have had money. The whole point about China until just the other day was that every one of them was equally broke and pathetic. Bunt hated doing business with upstarts, but of course they were all financial geniuses now, China was the country of the future, and they hadn't really spent forty-five years on their bony knees screeching socialist hymns and worshipping plaster statues of Chairman Mao.

In his baggy pants Mr Hung somewhat resembled Chairman Mao. That might have provoked his mother to make the deal. Betty despised Hong Kong but she despised China too. Selling the company and the site and clearing out was like an act of revenge on the workers (who she said were ungrateful) and on Mr Hung (whom she believed she was cheating). But Bunt also suspected that had she been pressed for a reason all she would have admitted by way of an explanation would have been, *Well, George was a snake, wasn't he?* or *My husband had an eye for the ladies, blast him.*

Worse than anything was Bunt's growing certainty that she took pleasure in the knowledge that he had been threatened. Her own threats never worked on him, but Hung had succeeded. Somehow, she knew: Mr Hung must have told her. What she had done eagerly, Bunt had done under pressure: she had been enriched, he had been broken. That he found hard to live with – his own mother gloating over his misery.

Now it was all done or nearly so – the details of the deal were being worked out.

In the meantime, Mr Hung insisted on celebrating. The Chinese businessman – was he? – seemed determined to host a party, yet it was premature, and inappropriate, for what Bunt felt more and more was the man's betrayal, which was something to regret. Bunt refused Hung's repeated invitations.

Everything had happened so quickly. One week he had met Mr Hung at the Cricket Club and turned his offer down flat. *Don't even think about it – you'll just make yourself miserable.* Less than a month later he had agreed to sell the company and, pending the setting up of a holding company in the Cayman Islands, he had all but signed. Imperial Stitching was his legacy, it represented his entire capital, in the only home he had ever known. In one stroke he was about to lose his company, his home, and his mother too – for only with the sudden death of Mr Chuck and the arrival of Mr Hung did he realize how much she had resented her husband, Bunt's father.

The prospect of the deal induced in him a mood of grief –

not the celebration Hung wanted. Bunt was still lugubriously enduring it. Later perhaps when the money was in his account he might raise a glass in a grim toast, but for now it seemed something to mourn.

Still he went to the office every day and what had seemed to him a monotonous duty became like a ritual of farewell which, as the days passed, made him sadder: he knew he was leaving the comforting walls of Imperial, and facing a future elsewhere. Bunt who had never lived anywhere but Hong Kong was leaving Hong Kong for good. And he was abandoning his workers, 'our family' Mr Chuck used to call them, leaving them to an uncertain fate, handing them over like the machines and the inventory of cloth and cotton reels.

Why was his mother so cheered by the idea of leaving? He did not know, but of course she had been raised in Balham, and she had worked at the Army & Navy, she had memories. London was real to her in a way that Hong Kong had never been. Perhaps that was it: she was going home, while Bunt was being cast adrift. The British in Hong Kong talked about Britain – 'UK' – often, but in a mood of insincere nostalgia, the way they reminisced about childhood or the war. Britain was like that, a dim memory that could never be verified or revisited.

Though they were glad to have it to talk about and were too loyal to mention that it was shameful and dreary, no one really wanted to go back to Britain. They had been liberated by Hong Kong, they had money and a sense of the exotic, they were superior here. Going home meant defeat – snubs and meagerness and middle-class making-do. The trouble was that the idea of England was easier to sustain the farther they were from the place.

These days in a mood of serving out an allotted span of time, Bunt kept away from his usual haunts. He was too sad. He did not want to be near the loud music, the hilarity, the persistent questions at the Pussy Cat. If he told Baby or any of the other Filipinos he was leaving for London they would want to go with him, and bring their family – mother, father, sisters, brothers.

Leaving the MTR subway station at Jordan one morning he bumped into the Mamasan. Seeing her in daylight was like seeing a lump of ectoplasm emerge from a parallel world – pale, pop-eyed, with claw-like fingers and a tentative way of walking.

'Why you no come to the club?'

He did not know what reason to give, because fear was the reason he felt.

'I'm sick,' he said.

It was the worst answer he could have given. The Mamasan looked at him sourly, as though he was the source of a dangerous infection, and she said no more. Her Chinese attitude towards disease, based mainly on superstition, verged on horror.

Mei-ping visited him discreetly in his factory office. She looked innocent and plain and even shapeless in her factory overalls and hair-net, but he knew the sweetness of her slender body and small bones, her pretty neck, her boy's bum.

'Yes?' he said, on his guard because she might have another message from Mr Hung.

'Do you want me?' she asked.

He had to say no. It made him sad to look at her, and he could not bear to hear her offer herself this way.

She hesitated but did not leave. She said, 'Can we go out to the pictures?'

Once they had seen a film together. *Lethal Weapon*. The violence had frightened her.

'Or music?'

Perhaps she was remembering the times he had taken her

to the Pussy Cat and they had sat there and watched the topless dancers; perhaps she knew that it had put him in the mood. But when had she ever so bluntly suggested it?

Bunt said, 'I don't feel well.'

'Maybe I can make you feel better.' She smiled, she winced: it was the same expression.

He was shocked by her directness.

'No problem,' she said.

It was what a bar girl in the Pussy Cat might say, encouraging him to step into a back booth, or a leering woman in a karaoke lounge. Perhaps he had had a hand in encouraging Mei-ping to behave like that? He had made this simple woman into a tart.

She went to the door but not to leave, only to close the door, then she dropped to her knees before him and looked imploringly up at him, slipped off her hair-net and let her black hair fall to her shoulders. Her face was upturned in submission.

Bunt struggled to move his legs together. He was so fuddled by Mei-ping that he motioned meaninglessly with his hands and said, 'Was there anything else?'

The kneeling woman was still staring hungrily at him.

'I need a passport, mister,' she said, and gripped him behind his legs, as though boarding a tram, using the vertically mounted handles beside the door.

Bunt was rigid, his knees went numb, his feet died. He had no way of securing a passport for her, or of speeding the lines at Immigration Tower.

'I'll try to see you right,' he said.

'You can help me, mister,' she said.

She touched him between his legs, and though it was affectionate, no more than teasing him, he reacted in terror, as though she had threatened him with castrating claws.

'Please,' he said, but could not manage anything else.

'Just saying hello to my friend,' she said.

Of all the many things that killed his desire, humor – and especially shallow jokes like this – flattened it the quickest and left it dead for a long time. He could tell her heart was not in it.

'So sorry,' she said. She now understood how badly she had misjudged him, and how she had failed.

She was lonely, she was desperate, she was clumsy and inept, and it was all his fault. When she finally left his office, her hair-net in her hand, he wanted to weep with frustration. And then, with her out of sight, he desired her, he wanted her back, he could not understand why he had rejected her. He hurried downstairs and into the street, to search for her. He saw her at the bus-stop with her friend from Cutting, Ah Fu. He wondered what Mei-ping had told her. The two young women, so sweet, so lost: Mr Hung had made him abandon them.

He said, 'Mei-ping, I wonder if I might have a word with you.'

'Not today,' she said. 'I have to go home.'

He deserved that for what he had put her through.

Driving home he detoured through Wanchai, telling himself that he was just looking, and seeing a parking place he stopped, telling himself that he was just curious. He found himself outside a club, La Bamba, advertising half-price drinks and no admission charge, and telling himself it was free, he went upstairs. The club was dark and loud music was playing. Various women approached him, saying hello. When his eyes grew accustomed to the darkness he saw a dozen Filipino girls dancing with each other to the music and beckoning to him. Bunt told himself that this never happened in Kowloon Tong, not so obvious as this, all those dark eyes and twitching buttocks he thought of as Hong Kong promises.

'What's yours?'

Backing away from the dance floor he was jostled towards the bar. He ordered a beer and was charged twice as much as it would have cost in the Pussy Cat.

'Hey, it's you again,' the man next to him said. 'Welcome to the Wanch.'

The man wore a black shirt and aviator sunglasses and stood with his elbows on the bar. His back was to the dancers, but perhaps he was looking at their reflections in the mirror behind all the whisky bottles.

Bunt said, 'Do I know you?'

'You're Monty's friend,' the man said, and groped at Bunt alarmingly at the level of his waist, trying to shake his hand. 'Hoyt Maybry.'

'I was just leaving,' Bunt said.

'Have a beer,' Hoyt said. He shouted, because the music was so loud.

'Thanks. I've got one.'

Still shouting – and the shouting made him sound insincere – Hoyt said, 'We don't have any of this in Singapore. You know our prime minister? Lee Kwan Yew? Hitler-with-a-heart, I call him.'

Bunt guzzled his beer. He hated drinking from the bottle, but Wanchai was the sort of district where it wasn't done to ask for a glass.

Hoyt said, 'Listen to your friend Monty. You should get yourself a new passport. Cape Verde Islands is a great one.'

'Thanks for the advice, but I'm not planning to renounce my UK citizenship just yet.' Bunt realized he sounded prissy as he said this, but the nerve of the man!

'I did it,' Hoyt said. 'And I'm an American.'

'I suppose it's ever so much harder for an American to chuck his passport.'

'You better believe it.'

Now Bunt was angry, and was edging away. It would not

be difficult to do in this darkness. He could not see the American's eyes through his dark glasses, but he could see the man's smile, and feeling self-conscious about starting to flee, Bunt tried to think of something to say, to fill the moment of awkwardness.

He said, 'What are you doing here anyway?'

'Bottom-feeding.' The man had not hesitated.

'Excuse me?' Before hearing the bewitching expression Bunt had seen only the swaying bottoms of Filipinos wearing blue jeans on the dance floor.

'This place is going to change a lot,' Hoyt was saying, gesturing in the dark. At first Bunt thought he was talking about La Bamba, but no. 'Hong Kong, with the Chinese running the show? Big changes.'

Americans ignorantly lecturing him on Hong Kong were just as numerous and only faintly less preposterous than Americans lecturing him on China. His mother just said, 'Yanks!' and laughed, but he had come to see them as dangerous bores and buccaneers.

'It doesn't much matter, does it?' Bunt said, because mentally he was beginning to move out.

'Sure it does. There'll be crime and corruption, back-handers all over the place, police on the take, child labor, pitiful wages, probably whore-houses up and down Central.' Hoyt sucked at his beer and said, 'All bargains. It'll be beautiful.'

The next day and for several succeeding days Mr Hung rang, to advise him of the progress of the deal – checks were being prepared, the name given to the new company account, Full Moon, was registered in the Cayman Islands – 'Where exactly are the Cayman Islands?' Bunt asked Monty, who had replied, 'On the Tropic of Cancer, I believe' – and Mr Hung repeated his invitation to celebrate the deal.

'Celebrate' meant summon witnesses, snap pictures, swap crummy presents, laugh insincerely, eat a revolting meal, close the deal, sign the paper.

'I'm busy,' Bunt said.

Sick, busy, helpless – those were his lame excuses, but the truth was sadder: he was dying inside, losing his business and his home, losing his mother, too, who had turned on him and on Hong Kong.

'Why not ask my mother?' he said. 'She likes a party.'

'This is between men,' Mr Hung said.

That meant he already had her signature.

And it also meant that instead of befriending his mother, who was grateful and would have enjoyed a chance to tell him stories, Hung had attached himself to Bunt, who resented him. It was as though, having proven Bunt to be weak, Hung now wanted to insinuate himself further, to exploit him more, to exhibit ownership, to toy with him, to savor the foreign devil's humiliation.

Without using the word – maybe he didn't know the word? – Hung seemed to want to subject Bunt to a binge. 'Must celebrate properly' was all he said, but Bunt knew what he meant: a bust, a blow-out, a knees-up, more. That was very English in some ways, Bunt felt; but it was Chinese too.

Something about feasting revealed a background of poverty and deprivation, where there was never abundance, where bingeing was infrequent and longed for, a dream fantasy of pleasure that was a kind of greedy madness, like drunks who sang themselves hoarse and stuffed their faces every Christmas until they spewed all over their shoes. Many of the English people in Hong Kong behaved like that. Bunt suspected his mother to be that way inclined until she said, 'People who do that sort of thing are common,' and then he was convinced of her passion for it, because, almost without exception, what she most yearned for she condemned.

'It's just so pig-ignorant to talk about money the way people here do,' she had been fond of saying before Mr Hung came along with his nine million Hong Kong dollars, each Honkers and Shankers banknote showing a lantern-jawed lion.

The repeated invitation to celebrate – 'tie one on' was the way Bunt interpreted it – would have indicated to any sensible person that Mr Hung was from a peasant family that had never known a good harvest. Mr Hung was from China. China was deprived. They were all like that, well-spoken but threadbare, polite but ruthless; they were civilized cannibals, who used napkins and had decent table manners but never the less flourished by sinking their teeth into you. Bunt would have been worried otherwise, for Mr Hung's good English did not hint at sophistication. He was simply better educated than the stiffs in Hong Kong, which was no distinction – the Colony's schools were appalling.

Mr Hung kept at it, calling him at work.

Bunt soon reached the point – which seemed inevitable to his browbeaten nature, especially when the other person was persistent – of knowing that eventually he would have to agree to some sort of party. Nagging succeeded with him where reason failed: it was his mother's doing. The only question was, what sort of party?

'If it's a banquet you're thinking of,' said Bunt, who was used to Hong Kong banquets – the tedium, the indistinguishable dishes, the waste, the transparent disguises of food, the fish heads, the pigs' feet, the spongy tripe, the tendons, fifteen courses of this glop were not unusual, 'any sort of banquet, you're wasting your time. Chinese food gives me a splitting headache.'

'Not a banquet, just we two,' Mr Hung said.

But that was as bad as a banquet: Bunt, feeling weak,

feared being near the man who had broken him. And Hung was so eager – that also made Bunt reluctant.

'Just a drink then,' Bunt said.

'More than one!' Mr Hung cried out.

A binge, in other words, for a Chinese person, any Chinese person, had two drinks and turned red and gasped and looked stricken and paralytic, with red puffy eyes and an expression of agony. The Chinese did not get drunk, they got sick – their livers couldn't process the alcohol – and it was not a pretty sight when they were struck down, struggling to ventilate, striking the belly-clutching postures of poison victims.

'I suppose I could meet you for a drink,' Bunt said, intrigued by his reverie of Hong Kong drunks.

If the drink was strong enough it would mean an early night, and when Mr Hung agreed Bunt began to relish the sight of the man lying on his side next to the bar, with a red swollen face, vomity froth on his lips, a blue tongue, and steam shooting out of his ears.

'By the way,' Bunt said, 'my Mum is getting a bit anxious about the deal.'

'I will bring you up to speed when we meet.'

When a person in Hong Kong used jargon correctly – especially American jargon – it was a sign that you had to proceed with caution.

EIGHT

Eager to have it over with, murmuring *Never again*, Bunt
arrived at the Regent early and stared across the busy harbor
at the Upper Peak Tram Station, his way of locating the
Peak Fire Station roof, and tracing the tree tops to Albion
Cottage. The sight of home calmed him. He was glad he
had got here first because of the chance it gave him to observe
Mr Hung, moon-faced and confused, entering the lobby bar.
In this glimpse, Bunt learned a little more about the man,
his awkwardness and impatience, his unfriendly way with
the waiters. Hung had a soldier's way of walking and an
officer's arrogance, as though he expected people to step
aside. But they didn't and it made him stumble and bat his
hands. What was he holding?

'There you are,' he said, seeing Bunt. Attempting to smile,
Mr Hung merely assumed an expression of greed.

Standing to attention, nodding slightly, he kept his hungry
look and tapped a cigarette on the case of his cellular
phone. His suit was the one he had worn at Fatty's
Chop-house, the label sewn on the cuff of his sleeve, his
new shirt was creased where it had been folded in the
box, his tie was badly knotted. His shoes were brilliant
black.

'Here I am,' Bunt said, looking at Hung closely. His father
had stood that way, he had seen men in clubs with that
posture. Hong Kong was a business center but it was also a

garrison – so many men had a military background. Bunt studied the way Hung carried himself and wondered, Had Hung ever mentioned the army?

'So good to see you again,' Hung said.

With his teeth clamped shut, Hung poked the buttons on his phone in a hard destructive way, as though putting out its eyes.

'I'm glad you started without me,' Hung said.

The Chinese man had mastered the insincere formalities of English, but what did it matter? He still looked like a snake and he spoke with menacing friendliness.

And in this new setting aspects of the man were revealed that Bunt had not noticed before. It was obvious here that Hung was a country mouse – so many of them were, the ones from China, and it showed in a comic way when they came to Hong Kong, especially in the bar of a luxury hotel. The man who was just a face in the crowd at Tsim Sha Tsui was lost here. No sooner had he tapped his cigarette on the cellular phone and started to light it, than the phone peep-peeped and he lost the call, juggling the instrument and finally dropping his cigarette. The waiter whisked it back into his hands, which made Mr Hung look more incompetent, because the waiter had acted with the sort of arrogant poise that looks deferential.

'I'm sorry, smoking's not allowed in this area,' the waiter said, looking pleased as Mr Hung frowned and stubbed the thing out.

'Brandy,' Mr Hung said.

Bunt was glad; alcohol was always toxic to the Chinese system, and Bunt wanted the pleasure of seeing the man stiffen and turn red and finally croak. Brandy! At six in the evening!

'Do you have a preference, sir?'

'The best,' Hung said, and that gave it away, the posturing, for only the most ignorant drinker would say that. 'The best' was a bumpkin's boast.

Bunt smiled, feeling superior at last, as Mr Hung shoved his cuff away from his watch, just a plastic watch, the sort of economy a Hong Kong Chinese would never make. Unwittingly drawing attention to its cheapness – it was little more than a toy, the sort of thing his mother called a pup – Hung kept looking at it.

The waiter brought his brandy in a snifter on a tray. Hung seized it and said, 'Cheers.'

As though impelled by a sudden thirst he drained the glass and was almost immediately rendered glassy-eyed. He squinted, his speech was slurred, and so, within minutes of arriving at the Regent he was simplified and blunted.

But the brandy also gave Hung a nastier face, and once again he looked to Bunt like a soldier, no longer an officer, he was now an enlisted man. Muttering numbers in Chinese he stabbed at the buttons on his cellular phone and got a busy signal. He cursed and looked around.

'Are you expecting someone?' Bunt asked.

Bunt had never seen him look so confused, but of course Hung was out of his element and that made a person impatient and restless, especially a man from China. The waiter attempted to speak to him in Cantonese, which Mr Hung did not understand; he spoke to him in English which he misheard, and it made the waiter smile and stare at him as though he were a dog who had learned a trick. Mr Hung would have fared better in a more pretentious place, where, in return for tips, the waiters were more forgiving and eager to please. But like the others who came from China Mr Hung had not learned that to get on in Hong Kong you had to hand out generous tips. Left to himself, among hostile or unhelpful waiters, Mr Hung seemed especially awkward and in his innocence he did not seem to understand that he was failing.

'I suggest that we drink up and then go,' Bunt said. 'I'd like to have an early night.'

Hearing a petitioning tone in his voice, he was annoyed with himself and also uncomfortably aware of his mind rushing forward to his mother in the badly lit lounge in the bungalow, reading tripe and waiting for him in her dressing-gown and fuzzy slippers. *I was seeing your friend Mr Hung, thanks very much, Mum.*

Bunt smiled angrily, completely in the dark as to why he was being kept waiting. So Mr Hung was asserting himself again, or was this just the random behavior of reckless boozing?

'They'll be here shortly, I expect,' Mr Hung said.

He spoke slowly, because he was drunk, but his drunkenness gave his manner of speaking even more precision. One of the most irritating Hong Kong experiences to Bunt was hearing someone he knew to be a complete bastard – someone he disliked, especially a Chinese businessman – speaking English correctly. He knew that proper English intimidated Americans in Hong Kong, but he had too much pride to attempt a posh accent.

Bunt had wanted the brandy to turn Mr Hung into an oik, but it merely made the man more pompous and tyrannical. Bunt refused to say anything more – why should he help Mr Hung hold a conversation? He tried to make himself drunk enough to ignore the situation, and to think of excuses to leave.

'Oh, there they are. Jolly good,' Mr Hung said.

Bunt looked up and saw a waiter guiding Mei-ping and Ah Fu through the lounge.

'You know each other?' Bunt asked.

Mei-ping bowed her head shyly. At such times she could look like a kitten – she had a simple feline face and soft skin, large eyes, no chin. Ah Fu smiled in apprehension. Bunt ruefully shared their nervousness, but for a different reason. His fears had been justified. Mr Hung had learned another of his secrets, an important one, making him weaker and Mr Hung stronger.

'We just happened to meet by chance,' Mr Hung said.

'At the factory,' Ah Fu said. 'Kowloon Tong.'

Ah Fu was pretty in a duck-like way, gabbled like a duck too, with a sort of Cantonese quack in her voice, and she looked around the lounge with her whole head turning on her long neck.

'Pure coincidence actually.'

Plonker, Bunt said to himself.

'He say you are his friend,' Mei-ping said.

What was odd and touching was the way in which Hung's fluent English allowed him to lie, while the women's plainer struggle with the language was so truthful.

'That you his partner,' Ah Fu said.

'In actual fact it's absolutely true, isn't it, Neville?'

It was the first time Hung had used his name, and it was so cruel the way he trotted it out, as though daring Bunt to deny it. Mei-ping his lover with whom he had been naked had never dared utter his name.

'Could be,' Bunt said, angry with Hung for everything now: the deal, the drink, the two women; subverting his mother, setting up his lover. Bunt was baffled by how Hung could possibly have known about Mei-ping. Hung had given her the blue jumper. The business in Jack's Place – *Your friend paid* – was easy to explain, since Bunt was a fairly regular customer. But Bunt had been careful to keep his relationship with Mei-ping hidden. Hung had found out. So Bunt was cautioned. Inviting Mei-ping and Ah Fu was Hung's way of intimidating him and boasting of his knowledge. How much more did he know?

94

'I'll have to be going soon,' Bunt said.

It was an ineffectual excuse. He wanted to escape. He wanted to hide. Yet he could not leave the two unsuspecting women with this man who had already insinuated himself into his life.

'After we eat,' Hung said.

It was what Bunt had feared most – Hung realizing his power and asserting himself.

'That's what I mean,' Bunt said, because there was nothing else he could say, and he sulked in the taxi all the way to the restaurant, jammed next to Mei-ping. He was aroused by her small nervous bird-bones quivering against his body.

A Chinese restaurant – and the name Golden Dragon was familiar – yet he had told Mr Hung more than once that he hated Chinese food, didn't eat it, hadn't touched it for years, because it gave him headaches and kept him awake. So why were they sitting in the Golden Dragon sipping tea while a waitress used tongs to offer them cold towels rolled and cased in plastic like sausages?

Hung meant to defy him. It was not subtle – they never were, anyway. It was where Hung had wanted to go when his mother had insisted upon Fatty's. Mr Chuck had eaten there. And, yes, in his ridiculously furnished flat with its white shag carpets and its silly glass case and absurd clock, Bunt had seen an ashtray labeled *Golden Dragon*, like the one here on this table. How appropriate that the Chinese businessman had stolen it.

Mei-ping and Ah Fu sat together, meekly whispering, while Hung held a menu and ordered the food. Bunt resented them now. How could he feel sorry for them? Their showing up was conspiratorial. Here were his trusted employees from Imperial Stitching – one of them his lover, sex partner anyway – helping Hung bully him.

Still rehearsing excuses, Bunt was imagining being brisk and businesslike with Hung – *'Talk to my lawyer – Monty will see you right . . . It's out of the question . . . I am afraid you are very much mistaken, Mr Hung . . . Well, you would say that, wouldn't you?'*

Mr Hung said, 'You're not paying attention, Neville.'

'Sorry,' Bunt said, and loathed himself for uttering the hated word.

The waiter stood smartly to attention taking down Hung's order on a pad, writing efficiently, and as he did so, repeating what Mr Hung was saying. After a moment, Bunt realized why Mei-ping and Ah Fu were uneasy. Mr Hung was addressing the waiter in Mandarin, not Cantonese. Although he could not speak either one, Bunt could distinguish between the two languages, the snarling twang of one, the goose-honk of the other, as different as a xylophone is from a lawnmower, and Cantonese was the lawnmower.

Hung dismissed the waiter abruptly, then looked at the young women. 'Did you understand what I said?'

Ah Fu giggled. Mei-ping said, 'Little bit.'

'Good for you.'

Wanker.

'And what did I order?'

Plonker.

'*Feng tsai*,' Mei-ping said. And to Bunt, 'Chicken feet.'

'But *feng* isn't chicken,' Hung said. '*Feng* is phoenix.'

'I knew that,' Bunt said. '*Yet lau, yet feng* – one room, one phoenix. It's an old tradition here.'

The local expression for a prostitute working on her own in Hong Kong, uttered by Bunt, caused Mei-ping to blush and giggle miserably at Ah Fu.

'These are chickens,' Hung said, when the food was brought. Six dishes were placed in the center of the table.

'Those are chickens too,' Bunt said. '*Gai dao* is a chicken house. Knocking-shop, we would say.'

Mei-ping covered her face in embarrassment while Ah Fu looked up to see whether anyone else in the restaurant heard what Bunt had said. Hung's merciless eyes were querying Bunt again.

'I was born here,' Bunt said. 'I know my way round.'

He knew perhaps a dozen words in Cantonese, which seemed to Bunt more than adequate. He had lived in the colony his entire life, and he was forty-three years old. Now he looked back and wondered. Of the many offenses Mr Hung had committed against him, one of the worst was that he had made Bunt reflect with bitterness on his life.

'I hope you are hungry,' Mr Hung said.

He had ordered all the dishes without consulting anyone else at the table, and even Bunt, who denounced Chinese food and never ate in such restaurants, knew that was bad form. But why should Hung care? For all their beauty, the two women were lowly factory workers, and Bunt was a prisoner.

'Chicken feet,' Mr Hung said. 'Phoenix feet.'

Hearing that, Bunt resolved that he would not eat, nor would he even pretend to. Not eating would be his protest and his rejection of the hospitality. He would defiantly remain sober, too, a condition which Mr Hung had abandoned. The man was grinning stupidly and almost drooling.

'What's funny?' Mr Hung said to the women.

They giggled on, chattering hard, their eyes fixed in manic fear.

'Sit near me,' Mr Hung said to Ah Fu. 'There, I am sure Mei-ping would be happier sitting with Neville.'

Though he hated the man for suggesting this, Bunt knew that to object would only expose him to greater ridicule.

'She can have my share,' Bunt said, for he saw Mei-ping picking at the cold dishes. What Bunt wanted to say was: *I don't think of this as food, and I would not even dream of putting it into my mouth.* When Mei-ping offered some to him he drew back, hoping that Mr Hung would see his expression of shock, and said, 'Of course not.'

Brandy was gleaming on Mr Hung's lips. He looked drunk, his face pinkish and raw, his eyes boiled, and he was smiling in a vicious way as he chewed with his mouth open. Bunt remembered the look of greed, of heedless hunger, he had seen on Hung's face in the lounge of the Regent. It was the desperate peasant who had been wrenched from his village and plonked down in luxury. He had not known that Bunt was staring at him: that was Hung's real face.

Hung said, 'These chicken feet are first quality. You appreciate them?'

He was speaking to Ah Fu as he examined a chicken foot, using his chopsticks like tongs and dangling the yellow foot in front of his watery eyes. Then he dropped it on to his plate and began to claw at it.

'I think so,' Ah Fu said shyly, her voice trailing off.

'Are you completely bewitched by them?' Hung's lower teeth showed as he set his jaw to tear off the chicken foot.

Ah Fu murmured to Mei-ping, who said, 'She says you speak English so well.'

Hung was hunched over the drooping foot, scraping at its yellow scales, dragging white tendon strings from its slender shank.

'In the future, we will teach you,' he said, gripping the chicken foot in his teeth.

Hung meant the Hand-over, the Chinese Take-away, now more than a year off. Bunt loathed the subject and when it came up always said, 'I don't even want to think about it,' and here he was, hating himself and listening to a Chinese man chewing and gloating over it.

'So many people will come to Hong Kong,' Mei-ping said. 'Chinese people.'

Hung was still chewing, flecks of leg scales on his lips, the chicken foot near his mouth as he gnawed, and still he replied, saying, 'Not necessarily.'

'They will take our jobs, we think,' Mei-ping said.

Hung looked at her sternly, like a teacher distracted by a commotion at the back of the class. He held the chicken foot upright in the grip of his chopsticks.

'That's what people say,' Mei-ping said. 'Because the Chinese are clever and well trained. They are also tough.'

'But we are rubbish,' Ah Fu said, chewing with a down-turned mouth.

Hung did not reply but instead went on cramming the chicken foot into his mouth, finishing it off with his teeth. He spat a knuckle of gristle onto his plate and reached for another chicken foot.

'Not to worry,' he said, and gnawed. His face was so contorted by his chewing that he seemed to have no eyes. 'We will teach you.'

Ah Fu had been picking and peeling the mottled skin from the chicken foot. Mr Hung's gruntings showed her how to work the skin free and she timidly thanked him.

Seeing her draw away from him, Hung thrust his face at her and said, 'I want to eat your foot.'

Bunt was disgustedly drinking a pint of beer, eyeing the table with resentment, the dishes of sticky pork and soggy and wilted lettuce, the black vegetables, the gray broth, the purple meat. On one dish of yellow meat was a severed chicken's head, its eyes blinded, its scalloped comb torn like a red rag.

Hung's elbows were out, his blue tongue showed as he

stuck his chopsticks into the dish of yellow meat and used them like pliers to grasp a fragment of chicken breast. Its white flesh was exposed when he left a bite mark on it, then he chewed and gagged and pursed his lips. Again, with a retching noise, he spat garbage onto the table.

'This is delicious because it has been strung up,' he said. 'You know how? Some string – tie it.' He made deft throttling and knotting gestures with his fingers. 'Truss it well and hang it for days. Let it air dry. Just dangle there.'

Bunt watched the man salivating as he spoke.

'It becomes tender and fragrant.'

Still salivating, he looked into the middle distance and apparently beheld the thing with his watery eyes, a suspended creature with a rope around its neck and its head flopped over. The apparition seemed to fill him with lust.

Bunt was frowning. Yes, the Chinese man had said, *I want to eat your foot.*

Drumming with his fingers on the table, Bunt was impatient. He had stopped being bored, he was now furious and wary, listening to the drunken man describe how a chicken should be trussed.

'Say something.'

It took a moment before Bunt understood that the man was speaking to him.

'I have nothing to say.'

Plonker, he thought. And, *What am I doing here?*

'My partner,' Hung said to Ah Fu, and when he touched her she stiffened inside her dress and got smaller. 'Here, I have something for you.'

Mr Hung searched his pockets and found a silk pouch, which he opened. He removed a piece of jade – small, dark green, a pendant perhaps. He held it before Ah Fu's face.

'Open your mouth.'

The young woman obeyed, her tongue twitching, and Mr Hung put it into her mouth. She pressed her lips together and worked it for a moment like a cough drop, then spat it into her hand and thanked him in a fearful voice.

Hung laughed and said, 'Where is the bitter melon?'

Hearing the insistent question, the waiter hurried over, walking in the jerky way he had all evening – nervousness, perhaps.

'I gave you instructions,' Hung said.

'Yes, sir.'

'Bitter melon,' he cried out. 'Are you stupid!'

Bunt was always puzzled hearing two Chinese people speaking to each other in English, but this was almost too much for him.

'Do you see any melon on this table?' Saying that, Mr Hung snatched a knife and added, 'Here, or here, or here?' He slashed repeatedly on the table for emphasis, leaving a narrow cut each time in the stained tablecloth.

'It was not served, sir,' the waiter said, examining the order pad with his finger. 'Very sorry.'

'If you didn't write it down, that's your problem,' Mr Hung said. 'Now stop arguing with me and bring it. I want it now!'

His mouth was open, gaping, full of yellow teeth and bits of metal and fragments of food. His tongue was discolored. His eyes were glazed, exhausted, red-veined, almost squeezed shut by the puffy flesh around them. His head was damp, his hair spiky.

He had perhaps not realized that several full minutes had passed since he had howled at the waiter. He turned his drunken face to Ah Fu and Mei-ping.

'Chickens,' he said, and slavered.

They were terrified, Bunt could tell. They deserved to be for being there at all.

'Where do you think you are going?' Mr Hung yelled in anger, just as he had spoken to the waiter, but before he could repeat it, Bunt had gone through the gold-painted moongate entrance and was out the door.

NINE

On the Star Ferry (the Rover wouldn't start, he had taken the Peak Tram and now he was crossing the harbor) the obscure suspicion that something was wrong nagged badly at Bunt. It was like the left-over derangement of a dream, as when he woke up flustered, in damp pajamas, with a taste of glue in his mouth, troubled by nameless blame. He had stolen something, he had broken something, he had given offense, he was hideously late. Blunders filled all his dreams. From the ferry rail he saw a Chinese bag of flimsy plastic ballooned and floating just beneath the surface with a sodden length of string. He wondered if it would snag on the ferry screws; and a shoe bobbing upside down – as though marking a drowning.

At breakfast his mother had said, 'What's wrong?' and that had only made it worse, because he suspected that something was seriously wrong, but he could not say what.

'See you letter,' he heard. It was a child's voice.

A man and woman sat in chairs by the rail with their small child between them.

'See you later,' the man said.

'See you letter,' the child repeated.

'And how are you?' the woman said.

'And how are you?' The child was excited, his voice was shrill.

'One, two, three, four, five, six,' the man said.

'One, two, fee, fo, fi, sick.' The child sang the numbers.

'See you later.'

'See you letter!'

Bunt would have been happier hearing them speaking Chinese. This English lesson was a reproach and under the circumstances it was futile. He walked to the stern, hating the chatter. He could not account for his uneasiness, yet he was sure that today something was distinctly different. He sensed an emptiness, as of something missing. There was this morning a small hole in the world and he had the uncomfortable notion that he had made the hole. It was worse than a hole, it was a leak.

Hong Kong was not home because Hong Kong was always strange to him, and so Bunt never spent a day in the colony without feeling that he was partly inhabiting a dream. His dreams were familiar only as foreground and the rest was foreign; his dreams were cloudy, and fuzzy at the edges. He flew in his dreams with his arms out, but he seldom knew what country he was flying over, and he never landed. Often, leaving Kowloon Tong and work, and entering the bungalow at night, seeing his mother, he had the impression that he was just waking to reality after a day of abstraction. The city's bad air and confusion and odd accusatory noise kept him indoors. *I live here. I will not die here*, he told himself. It was the only place he had ever lived in, and yet Hong Kong was not home. Home was a larger warmer word. Perhaps Albion Cottage was his home, but his mother crowded it.

Just the fact today that his car would not start added to his anxiety. He had an inkling that the truth would be revealed – someone would tell him what was wrong. He hoped his dream, whatever it had been, was misleading and that he was not responsible.

Approaching the Imperial Stitching building he noticed

that the Union Jack was not flying from the factory flagstaff. Its absence gave the building a colorless look, even a meekness, as of surrender.

'Mr Woo did not come to work today,' Miss Liu explained.

Bunt could not remember a time when Mr Woo the janitor had been absent from work. In fact, since 1984 Mr Woo had made a point of being punctual in raising the flag, as though making a statement against the Hand-over. Mr Woo it was who refused to speak the name of the dictator of China – Bunt did not know the man's name so it made little difference. Mr Woo had a nickname for the man, and anyone within earshot giggled when Mr Woo referred to him as 'The Turtle's Egg.'

'Is Mr Woo the only person who knows how to run up the flag?' Bunt said.

Miss Liu hesitated. Apparently the answer was yes.

'Isn't it time someone else learned?' Bunt demanded.

The task – with the rest of Mr Woo's custodial duties – was assigned to Winston Luck, in Shipping, until Mr Woo returned.

Mr Woo's absence, like the Rover that wouldn't start, only added to Bunt's sense of disquiet.

Towards noon, as Bunt was going over the production figures for the previous month – Mr Chuck would have been pleased, he thought with a pang – Monty Brittain phoned to say that he needed Bunt's signature on some Full Moon documents, and could Bunt meet him for a late lunch at the Hong Kong Club?

'Done,' Bunt said.

Might this provide the revelation he had been waiting for ever since he left the house? Whatever, he felt rescued by the call. He knew that he had to remain fully awake and watchful. The answer was somewhere out there.

He was even now vaguely rattled by Monty's having told

him that he had renounced his British citizenship and was now an Austrian. That his name was Brittain made the whole business seem peculiar, and Bunt remembered that when Monty had revealed it, whispered the word 'Austrian,' he'd had a beer stein in his hand and suds on his mustache.

The image would not fade. It was just a tax-saving ploy, Bunt knew that. Monty had no intention of retiring to a suburb of Vienna; he could not see the Jewish solicitor wearing leather pants and one of those silly trilbies and listening to an oompah band, all farting trumpets and snare drums, with a men's choir shouting the sort of German folksong that always sounded like 'Shtick your finger up your bum!'

Monty, an Austrian. That was strange, perhaps even stranger than the opinionated American with the African passport who called himself 'a bottom-feeder.' Perhaps it was all the result of living in Hong Kong, in a fury of activity in which any sort of transformation seemed possible.

Still, Bunt set off for lunch in an expectant mood, glad of the chance to talk to someone sympathetic. He was grateful for Monty's call, because Monty knew Hung and would listen to his anxieties. It had been an awful night, all that business with Hung and the chicken feet at the Golden Dragon. After the revolting meal Bunt had gone home and on entering Albion Cottage he saw his mother in her robe and slippers, waiting up like a wife. Kissing him, she had leaned over and loudly sniffed and made a face. She often did that in the evening, in an abrupt scrutinizing way, like a quality control inspector wrinkling her nose, saying nothing, yet radiating disapproval.

Bunt said, 'I was with your friend Hung again.'

'I'm sure.'

Trying to be superior and haughty always made her ridiculous. The poor woman had a Form Four education. She often joked about it, 'Thick as two short planks,' she said, and sometimes it was, 'Well, I'm a graduate of the College of Short Planks.' She was never so withering as when she was earthy, repeating the vulgar folk-wisdom of her parents. She could say, 'He's from the gutter,' with the authority of someone who knew the gutter.

'We were at a Chinese restaurant,' Bunt said. 'I didn't eat anything. I drank two beers, made my excuses and left.'

'Of course you did.'

Her sarcasm grated, because it was witless, because he deserved better. To have endured such a night was bad enough, but for his mother to dismiss it – sniffing, sneering, frowning in his face as though she had a bad smell in her nose – this was worse.

'Mum!' he complained.

'You are humming with Woman,' she said. 'I smell Tart.'

'Mr Hung's friends.'

He had taken a dislike to Mei-ping and Ah Fu for accepting the invitation. They should have known better even if Hung had not. Who did they work for? Who paid their salaries? And there was Ah Fu from Stitching, opening up and letting this awful man stick a piece of jade into her mouth. A Chinese custom, perhaps, but he wanted no part of it.

'I'm sure,' his mother said and went back to her armchair and her newspaper, ostentatiously holding it up and rattling the pages to screen her face from him.

To be accused of lying when he was telling the truth made him feel violent, because in this instance words were no use – she had stopped listening. He wanted to break something – not to hit her but to smash something and frighten her; just to fling one of her ugly duty-free-shop souvenir saucers against the wall.

But if he had, what would happen? His mother would crumple and contract in fear. She would cry and she would win – though she shouted like a navvy, she blubbed like a little girl. Wang would emerge from his room and silently, reproachfully sweep up the pieces. And he would spend a week or more being reminded that he had hurt her feelings – and he would be in the wrong.

'Wang's made you a hot drink.'

'No thank you.' That was his protest – that and the snub of going to bed before she did.

When she referred to it in the morning – wrinkling her nose, making a face, sourly smacking her lips – he realized how she must have done that very thing with his father many mornings when she had suspected him of being with his Chinese mistress, the Mamasan. He forgave his mother, for she had suffered the humiliation of her husband's infidelity. How it must have pained her. Though, on reflection, he wondered whether she had driven him to it.

But what have I done? It seemed so unfair that he should be blamed, that he was not trusted.

He said, 'I hate that man Hung.'

'What does it matter?' she said. 'He's doing business with us. If he pays top whack as he promised, I'm not bothered.'

'I think he's a beast.'

The word tumbled out – he had not rehearsed it. He was startled by the accuracy of what he had said. *Beast* summed him up.

'He's buying the company,' his mother said, as though Bunt's statement was irrelevant.

Perhaps it was irrelevant. If Hung had been a faceless buyer, just a name on a document, he would not have mattered. But he wasn't faceless, he was a beast, and so wasn't that a factor? That awful bottom-feeding Yank had said, *Basically the Chinese are giving you the finger the whole time*.

Bunt said, 'I'd like to beat him to jelly.'

'Steady on, Bunt. You'll do nothing of the kind.'

'I wish Mr Chuck were still alive.'

The old man had been a father figure. Having repudiated China, he had become self-sufficient in Hong Kong, with the unvarying consistency of the refugee: sticking to his principles, making sacrifices, working hard, being thankful. Mr Chuck's contempt for China was undisguised. China was a prison, Chairman Mao was a Turtle's Egg. Mr Woo, who occasionally served as Mr Chuck's driver, had learned the insult from him. Bunt missed Mr Chuck for the hope and stability he had represented. And he had liked him even more when he had glimpsed him in the Pussy Cat.

'Poor Henners,' his mother said. 'But if Henry Chuck were still alive you'd be a lot poorer.'

'None of this would have happened,' Bunt said. 'Since he died, everything's changed.'

And he went outside and could not start the Rover. It seemed like another aspect of a pattern of uncertainty and loss. Then no Union Jack, no Mr Woo. With such dread on his mind everything looked like an omen of dwindling possibilities.

Monty was waiting for him in the Hong Kong Club foyer, under the portrait of the Queen. He unzipped his briefcase as soon as he saw Bunt.

'Should I have signed you in, squire?'

'No,' Bunt said. 'I'm still a member. I don't know why. I never use it.'

'I know why. It's because the waitresses aren't topless,' Monty said. 'Sorry. Bad joke, squire.'

He had quickly apologized because Bunt's face had darkened. But Bunt was ashamed of himself. So that was how he was thought of, as a regular at the chicken houses and karaoke bars and the topless clubs and blue hotels. What made it all the more pathetic was that he lived with his mother.

'That's me,' Bunt said, 'another gweilo whore-hopper.'

'Not at all,' Monty said, being brisk to cover his embarrassment, pulling a file of papers from his briefcase. He went on, 'We'll have to deal with this here. It's forbidden to transact business in the Jackson Room. Club rule, as you no doubt recall.'

Monty seemed pleased to be reminding Bunt of this, the oddity and inconvenience of it. It was something expatriates seemed to relish, and Bunt, who was not an expatriate but rather Hong Kong born and bred, regarded it as pure foolishness, that worst of English traits, eccentricity for its own sake, making a vice into a virtue, a maddening nuisance into something lovable.

'Stupid rule,' Bunt said, as he signed the papers headed *Full Moon (Cayman Islands) Ltd*. 'I reckon that's why I never come here. I mean, you can transact business at Bottoms Up, what?'

'Very British,' Monty said.

'That's what I mean,' Bunt said. 'But aren't you supposed to be German?'

'Austrian,' Monty said. 'But do keep your voice down, squire. That's supposed to be hush-hush.'

They went upstairs to the Jackson Room, Monty greeting other members on the stairs.

'Get out while you can,' one man was saying.

'Nonsense, this is a great time to be here,' his partner replied.

'Quite right,' Monty said, genial again.

After they were shown to a table, Monty leaned over and said, 'Austrian passport. It's not quite the same thing as being an Austrian.'

'I must be stupid,' Bunt said.

'Is everyone who carries a British passport British?' Monty asked.

'I should jolly well hope so,' Bunt said. He sulked for a while, wondering what had happened to his mood – he had been looking forward to this lunch. He looked around the crowded restaurant, the murmuring diners in their dark suits, nearly all gweilos, and at a waiter trundling a trolley of bleeding beef. Then he said, 'Monty, I want to finish this business.'

'Soon, squire, don't you worry. The third company is registered. I've prepared the documents.' Monty was sipping a gin and tonic. 'Are you sure you don't want a new passport?'

'I've got a passport.'

'Something a bit more convenient than the standard UK issue.'

'Austrian?'

'Squire,' Monty pleaded and became businesslike again. 'Cayman Islands is a good bet. Or you could become an American.'

'Me – a Yank!'

'Non-resident, squire,' Monty said. 'It makes all the difference.'

'No bloody fear of that,' Bunt said, and muttered, 'Yank? I met your Yank friend the other night. Is that an act or is he trying to be colorful the way they do sometimes?'

'Hoyt made a million US by getting himself a new passport. You don't have to, but you ought to consider taking a year off – drop out for a tax year. A spell in Monaco or even Ireland would save you an awful lot of money.'

Bunt put his face forward and said, 'Monty, I was thinking I might stay right here in Hong Kong.'

'Under the terms of the conveyancing agreement that is out of the question. You have to leave.'

'Who's to know?'

Bunt smiled and said no more until he had ordered his lunch and the waiter had moved off.

Monty said, 'I've done some spade-work, squire. I know a bit more about our Mr Hung.'

'I hate him,' Bunt said without feeling. 'He's awful. He's a spotty bottom. I told him so.'

'It needed to be said.' Monty was smiling, as though there was something admirable in Hung's awfulness. 'I checked his credentials. They're all in order.'

Falling silent while the salads were set out and the black pepper ground on them, Monty resumed as soon as the waiter was out of earshot.

'He's PLA – an army officer,' Monty said. 'He already has some of his troops installed at Stanley.'

Bunt said, 'It really amuses me that the Chinese call their soldiers the People's Liberation Army.'

'Is that sillier than calling them Beefeaters?'

'I don't know,' Bunt said. 'Austrians call their chaps Storm Troopers, don't they?'

'You're thinking of Germans – world of difference,' Monty said, looking pained. 'I wish I had never told you of my difficult decision.'

Bunt was on the verge of apologizing when he looked across at Monty and thought: *Leather trousers, trilby hat, farting trumpets, oompah band, 'Shtick your finger . . .'*

'Your Mr Hung has an inkling that you are not in total sympathy,' Monty said. 'Which is why he is stipulating that one of the conditions of the sale of your factory is that you leave Hong Kong for good.'

'What if I don't want to leave?'

'He is in a position to see that you do – to show you the door, smartish,' Monty said. 'He may look a fool, but he could prove a formidable opponent.'

Chewing lettuce, crunching it and facing Monty, Bunt

said, 'I never said he was a fool. I said he was a wanker.'

'A nice distinction,' Monty said. 'One of the clauses in the document you just signed affirms your agreement to leave Hong Kong in order to collect the proceeds of your sale, and in any case before June, 1997, whichever is sooner.'

'Why didn't you tell me?'

'I am telling you now, squire,' Monty said. 'That's why I asked you here.'

'Knickers,' Bunt said.

The pork chops were served, the roast potatoes, the sprouts. Dessert was flan. He felt he was giving himself indigestion. He had thought he might discover something from Monty that would ease his mind, and yet all that lunch had done was make him more disturbed. Hung was not just a beast but a powerful beast, and a wanker, too.

'You want to be careful, squire,' Monty said, and tapped the side of his nose to give his statement significance. 'You know about Feetly?'

Over coffee in the Garden Lounge – Monty was waiting for his wife who, being a woman, was not allowed into the Jackson Room – elbows on knees, all confidential, Monty told Bunt the story of a Hong Kong lawyer named Feetly. Feetly fell in love with a Chinese prostitute he had met in a club in Mong Kok. Bunt listened carefully: he was often in the Mong Kok clubs himself.

Helplessly infatuated, Feetly had pursued the woman, buying her favors and monopolizing her time, until the gang of snake-heads that ran her shipped her back to Shanghai.

Feetly followed with a suitcase full of money, in an attempt to buy her freedom. With the connivance of the prostitute Feetly was invited to a meeting to discuss the matter, and he was killed. The money was stolen, of course, but the money was not the issue. Feetly's body, chopped into pieces, was found in a conspicuous steel drum labelled *Hazardous*

Material and left just over the frontier, near a border fence in a *bok choi* cabbage field at Lok Ma Chau. It was a message to anyone else who might be inclined to mistake whoring for courtship, or who doubted the authority of the Chinese.

'It's a Chinese tragedy,' Bunt said.

Monty said, 'I think of it as a Hong Kong love story.'

'I know better than to fiddle with the triads,' Bunt said.

'Who said anything about the triads?' Monty said. 'It was the Chinese army who killed him. They own half the massage parlors in Shenzhen. Next year they will be operating here. I am speaking of your Mr Hung.'

Bunt was silent, and then he remembered how they had first met. He said, 'How did he become a member of the Cricket Club?'

'I proposed him,' Monty said, and before Bunt could respond, added, 'You've got to move with the times.'

Bunt nodded. He gave the impression that he was not overly concerned. Yet he was convinced. Monty had said enough. Bunt said nothing more so as not to reveal that he was terrified.

Soon after, Mrs Brittain arrived at the Garden Lounge and was escorted to their table by the waiter. She was tiny, brittle-looking, fastidious. She said *Helew!* in a Home Counties neigh and said she was parched and would have *a glass of drai whait wayne*, and how was Betty Mullard? Bunt replied but distractedly, for he could not get over the fact that her husband had made Mrs Brittain an Austrian, for goodness' sake. He saw the little woman in leather pants, among tankards of beer and chunks of cheese, as a band played among garlanded tanks.

Lunch had left him dazed – the salad, the pork chops, the pint of beer, the rich dessert, the news that Hung was powerful. The food at first had filled him and made him indifferent, and so when Monty told him about Hung he was confused. Then it sank in. He now needed solitude, to reflect on what Monty had said. The heavy meal put him in a stupor – he was anxious but helpless.

Standing at the Star Ferry terminal he remembered the small child that morning chanting *See you letter* and counting *One, two, tree, fo, fi, sick*. The useless English lesson.

On the Kowloon side he walked past the buses and taxis and wandered the maze of streets near Hankow Road as far as Haiphong Road, where he cut through the park, still fretting and swallowing the bad air. All the while he looked into shop windows and at people's faces, thinking that the answer to his dilemma might lie on this route. But he felt nothing except greater unease, almost despair, when at last he boarded the MTR and rode from Yau Ma Tei to Kowloon Tong.

It was late, almost four-thirty, when he got off the elevator to enter his top-floor office. Mei-ping stood at the elevator door. How long had she been there? He had never seen her waiting like that.

She was expressionless. Bunt invited her into his office. As soon as the door was closed she lost her composure and began to speak, her voice distorted by a screech of panic.

'Ah Fu never came home last night!'

He motioned with his hands for her to lower her voice. Next door Miss Liu had to be listening. Lily and Cheung were not far away either.

Bunt said, 'She was with her friend Mr Hung, wasn't she?'

Bunt was cross. Mei-ping had disturbed his anxious reverie, making him more anxious. How could he think with her screeching like this?

'I wait last night. I wait today. Ah Fu not come to work today,' Mei-ping said. Her face was pale and swollen with grief, the bloodless color of a steamed bun.

Bunt said, 'I think she is where she wants to be. Excuse me.'

Trying to get past her, to enter his inner office, he remembered his resentment at seeing the two women arriving at the Golden Dragon. It was a cruel trick for Mr Hung to invite them. And they had cooperated – oblivious of the embarrassment they had caused Bunt. They had helped Mr Hung remind Bunt that he had no more secrets. They had sat and listened to Mr Hung calling him Neville.

Though she looked abject Mei-ping stood her ground, blocking Bunt's way, and said, 'I worry.'

She seemed to him obstinate and devious and he wanted to push her over.

'Go back to your machine,' Bunt said. 'Surely there's some stitching that wants finishing?'

That was all it took to make her sag and drop her head and turn away. Bunt watched her go. He heard her descending the stairs. He heard the clacking of the machines blare as the stitching room door opened and shut. In his office Bunt looked at the sales figures again. He held the paper to his face but could not read them: he felt demented. He was now angry with Mei-ping – her insolence, her useless grief, her interruption: another problem, another omen.

Then something took hold of his mind and pinched it as though a pair of claws had pierced it and hung on where it was the most tender. He began to murmur *yes, yes*. The vanishing of Ah Fu was not an omen. It was the dreaded event of his bad dream.

He called the floor supervisor and asked for Mei-ping to be sent to his office.

'I am sorry to make you angry,' Mei-ping said.

'I am not angry,' he said. He was calm as he spoke, and for the first time that day he felt he was not going insane. 'Tell me why you are worried.'

Mei-ping paused and took a breath and exhaled and said, 'After you left us last night I was feeling so bad. I want to go home and forget.' She paused and breathed a little. 'Mr Hung say he want to take us to dancing. I say no. Ah Fu say no.'

She was silent a moment, not stumped, just pausing, going at her own speed. She was confident of what she wanted to say.

'Mr Hung say to me, that, "Go." Mr Hung take Ah Fu.'

All these misters and he was such a beast.

'Dancing?'

'I don't know. She never come home.'

'Don't worry,' Bunt said, thinking again: This is what I needed to know.

'I worry.'

Bunt said, 'She might be very happy.'

There was not the slightest indication in Mei-ping's expression that this could be the case.

'I'll find out,' Bunt said. 'I'll call him.'

'Maybe call the police,' Mei-ping said.

After what Monty had told him of Hung's influence, Bunt knew that this idea was to be resisted. Bunt ceased being a sympathetic listener and assumed the role of Mei-ping's employer.

'I will handle it,' he said. He stood up to indicate to Mei-ping that it was time for her to leave. 'You can go home.'

Was it the word 'home'? Whatever, it triggered a flood of tears – sobs which convulsed her. It was as though she was giving birth to a monster, and frantic with the pain she staggered away in the midst of her labor. Her small body heaved as she carried her grief out of the door and down the hall. Her weeping was audible from the enclosed elevator and Bunt could hear her sobs descend to the street; and soon they were outside the window where, after a moment or two, they were extinguished by all the other howling in the din of Kowloon Tong.

Bunt had woken that day with the inarticulate suspicion that something was wrong, and now he knew what it was. He was not happy, but he felt a sharp sense of relief, a new vitality that had been brought on by a significant disclosure: he had found the thing he had searched for the whole day. Ah Fu was missing: that was the event that had unsettled his mind, that he needed to be told. It had been like a bad smell. He had now found the source of the odor. He was proud of himself.

He mentioned it to his mother that evening.

She dropped her knitting into her lap. She sucked at the surface of the tea in her cup. She said, 'We managed to live here as long as we have by not asking about matters that didn't concern us.'

Bunt said, 'And she didn't show up at work.'

'There was always something,' Betty said, still generalizing over her teacup. 'The bally war. The Mao business. The bally students when they didn't want the British here. The first lot of riots. The second lot – just Chinky-Chonks flinging dustbin lids, but there it is. How many murders? How many busts? And the police – nancy-boys, blackmail, backhanders, drugs, packets of beastly photographs. We kept out of that, too. Let them get on with it. The boat people and now this bally Hand-over. We got through it all because we didn't want to know.'

Bunt said nothing and yet his mother knew that his mind was teeming.

'If you don't want to know, you're not bothered,' she said, and seeing that Bunt was about to speak she added quickly, 'Don't tell me her name.'

Bunt sat down to dinner – Wang's shepherd's pie and

baked beans; sprouts; trifle; remaining silent, just chewing. Ruminant, he seemed on the verge of speaking, but he was holding back.

From her chair, where she had resumed knitting, Betty said, 'And don't go to the police.'

He slept badly. In the morning, once again the Rover would not start, but that was no longer an omen, nor was the ferry rolling in the wake of a freighter, the oil slick in the harbor, the buoyant garbage, the staring passengers – none of it was ominous now. He knew what was wrong, but how to fix it?

Mei-ping was waiting at his office door, wearing a pious look of suffering.

'You call the police, mister?'

'I made some inquiries.'

Mei-ping seemed to know instantly that it was a lie.

'Why you not call police, mister?'

'Because Ah Fu might be with her family.'

'She have no family here. Only me. You can see Mr Hung?'

Bunt said, 'We can't go around accusing people of crimes.'

He did not want to speak with Hung. He could not dial the number. He held back, not knowing what it was that was keeping him in check. Was it fear? Monty's story of cruelty and revenge on the Hong Kong lawyer, the man's chopped-up body in a steel drum, cautioned him.

There was the possibility – perhaps the certainty – that the Imperial Stitching deal would be soured by any inquiry. Even asking Hung about Ah Fu's disappearance would be a mistake. The Chinese were not subtle, nor were they casual in anything they did. One word would spoil everything; and his mother, who had not only mentally moved out of Hong Kong but had also mentally moved into a substantial double-fronted Edwardian house on the promenade at

St Leonards-on-Sea, would blame him for the failure if it failed.

His fear that Mei-ping was right, and that Mr Hung was responsible for the disappearance of Ah Fu, also kept him from wanting to know more. If there had been a crime, what then?

TEN

His mother was no help – Bunt put it down to insecurity and envy. Saying, 'Leave it alone,' she seemed to be challenging him to defy her. As the years had passed – he blamed Hong Kong, her isolation on the Peak – she had begun more and more to use such occasions as tests of her son's loyalty.

Although as a final flourish she lifted her meddling head like an empress, she had an old woman's turtle face, all stringy neck and beaky in profile, which gave her the strangely vulnerable and pathetic look of an endangered species.

What was implied but remained unspoken was the suggestion, *If you are true to me you will obey.*

'Mr Hung,' she said, apparently thinking out loud, and she smiled and squinted, as though summoning up his face. 'Even if someone tells you in a lot of fiddly detail what a Chinese person has on his mind – even then you will never understand.'

Bunt stared at her, hearing only, *Obey me.*

'When I was a girl we always used to say, "He's out of his tiny Chinese mind." That means something, Bunt.'

It meant she never became involved with anyone in Hong Kong and indeed, though she descended the Peak to gamble at Happy Valley or Sha Tin, or to shop, to bank, or have tea in a hotel lobby or lunch in the Red Room at the Hong Kong Club accompanied by someone like Monty, her circle was English and she would not take the Chinese seriously.

The Chinese were successful in business because they kept their shops open until midnight and because they were desperate refugees. Unlike the British they had no hobbies, no recreations, no pleasures. Their gambling was purely self-destructive. 'Too weedy for sports.' The British held to their custom of civilized hours and early closing, half-day on Wednesday, weekends off. The British were rulers, the Chinese were their subjects. When had the subject peoples of the British Empire ever been anything but riddles? The Chinese were a supreme and slitty example of that. They were always out of focus, and the nearer you got to them the harder they were to see.

'I'm not bothered,' Betty said.

After more than fifty years the Chinese in Hong Kong had receded, becoming more numerous and more difficult to understand until they were now a total mystery.

'Chinese fire drill. Chinese checkers. It's all Chinese to me,' she said with a crooked smile that said, *And you should not be bothered.*

Mei-ping straining at his other ear at the factory demanding to know why Ah Fu had vanished was another burden for Bunt. She said she was afraid of the police.

His mother had perhaps suspected that there was something romantic in his relationship with Mei-ping – she knew much more than she said, it was her way of dominating him, he knew that. But he imagined her refusing to think about it, except as a reckless accident for which there could be no apology or explanation. If anyone were to be held accountable it was Mei-ping. They were all opportunists, Chinky-Chonks. Panicky Chinese were capable of any excess, and as they hunted for a passport, or a meal ticket, or a way out, they were all reaching hands and twitching fingers.

Yet that was not the way Mei-ping seemed to Bunt. In just two days Mei-ping had become beautiful. It was the effect of her sadness. Grief inhabited her and made her attractive. Bunt was ashamed of his tremulous interest, seeing her gaunt face and the depth of her dark and tearful eyes. Sorrow gave her a compliant posture, and a slight limp, and Bunt could not resist clutching at her when she appeared in his office, lamenting the disappearance of Ah Fu. She was fragile and sweet and unresisting – too bewildered to be suspicious. Bunt wanted to lick her tears off her hollow cheeks and to kiss her sadly pouting lips.

On the pretext of comforting her Bunt held her and stroked the soft flesh beneath her thin blouse. His fingers pressed to her bones, and he snorted with desire and murmured.

'Everything's going to be all right – trust me.'

Terror had stripped her of her manners and given her nerve. She was oddly bold one moment, and cowering the next. The other workers at Imperial Stitching seemed afraid of her, the way she approached Bunt – slamming the gates of the elevator, or hurrying up the stairs to his office without an appointment. She stared at him, sometimes calling out, 'Ah Fu!' She looked radiant.

Bunt kept seeing chicken feet and kept re-playing the ridiculous monologues of Mr Hung.

This is delicious because it has been strung up . . . Truss it well and hang it for days . . . Let it air dry. Just dangle there . . . It becomes tender and fragrant . . .

And his gloating red-eyed moan, *I want to eat your foot.*

Four days after the dinner at the Golden Dragon – four days since Ah Fu had vanished – Mei-ping met Bunt on the stairway when he arrived for work, with a pair of scissors in her hand. She had leapt from her work station as he had passed the open door.

'I want to go to the police station,' she said.

He could see that she did not want to do this at all, but that she was terrified and desperate.

'That won't help,' he said. 'What will the police do?'

'I will make a report,' Mei-ping said, her voice breaking. 'For the files.'

The word 'report' made Bunt see a useless sheet of official notepaper, bearing the seal of the lion and the unicorn, blown out of Mei-ping's helpless hands and boosted into the Hong Kong sky by a gust of wind and sailing away as it tore apart. Couldn't she see it too?

'They will put it into the window,' she said.

What was she talking about?

The incomprehension on Bunt's face seemed to goad her to greater insistence, but a moment later she broke and began to cry. She cried miserably, screwing up her face, pushing her swollen eyes with the backs of her fists. The scissors in her hands made her seem harassed and distracted rather than violent, though Bunt wished she would put them down and cry more compactly. There were tears on the scissor blades, tears on her chin, a snail-trail of snot on her sleeve.

'Please go to Mr Hung,' she whimpered.

Bunt was moved. There was nothing subtle in her weeping and the drama of it shook him – whipped at his desire and cracked his heart and roused him. Her body was contorted, crippled by the seizure of her tears. The whole business seemed urgent now – the thought of his mother saying, 'I'm not bothered,' annoyed him. His mother would never understand – she did not know enough of Mei-ping, and would never know.

A sad passion had also been part of his memory of their secret meetings in his office, or in the stockroom where they had lain on bolts of new cloth; and once in the Pussy Cat, where she had been shocked by the topless Filipinos, and many times in the blue hotels of Kowloon Tong. Some of those times her face had been smeared in tears, out of confusion or panic or the shame of her own desire. And though she had asked nothing of him she made love to him in a number of ways, even sitting on him and pretending to make him submit, it was her begging postures that drove him wild.

'I will see Mr Hung,' Bunt said.

It strengthened him to know that in seeing Mr Hung he was defying his mother. The rebellion was something new in him, seemingly triggered by Mr Chuck's death and the agreement to sell the company. It was related to Hong Kong most of all; all this business in Kowloon Tong meant that he would soon be homeless in the last days of the colony. He was angry. Lately, disobeying his mother filled him with conviction, because it isolated him and because it forced him to be cautious.

Had his mother allowed it or encouraged him or even taken a mild interest, the inquiry would have been casual. But she wanted him to obey her. She disliked Mei-ping. She had a contemptuous regard for Mr Hung: *He's someone I can do business with*. Her disapproval made Bunt secretive and intense and he guessed in advance that opposing his mother might help him to be effective. It made him fonder of Mei-ping, as though demanding the obedience his mother had forced him to choose.

Long ago, as a skinny and self-conscious pupil at Queen's – his mother always lingering by the gate after school – he had had a friend named Corkill who was just as disliked and bullied by the others as Bunt. The two boys sat together in the school yard, listening to the clang of trams in Causeway Road and whispering, sharing fantasies, usually sexual. Their joint fantasy was to be rich and to live in a big country house in Wessex (they were reading *Jude the Obscure*) with a Chinese nymphomaniac who had long red fingernails and a see-through nightdress, drinking champagne and rutting by the hearth fire and licking her 'amplitudes' (that was in the Hardy novel too).

Illicit and luxurious, it was Bunt's secret dream for many years. Corkill was small and spotty, ashamed of his father, who was a policeman, while at the same time pitying Bunt, whose father was dead. All that term, in the school yard they added details of the Chinese nymphomaniac, who was a princess and a whore. They tantalized each other, imagining tickle fights and forbidden words and perversities. It was a vision of paradise. Corkill said, *Spy on her when she's in the bog, Nev!* and Bunt said, *Pull down her knickers, Corky!*

Later, as an adult, Bunt sometimes found himself searching for this woman in the Pussy Cat or Jack's Place or Fat-Fat Chong, and he wondered what Corkill was thinking. Corky was back in the UK, probably married, with kids, and pretty miserable, while Bunt still dreamed.

'Jumper weather,' his mother called out, as he bolted his breakfast, setting off to see Mr Hung. She clapped his raincoat into his hand and poked an umbrella at him – her umbrella, he saw, and was irked. She said, 'Gamp. Don't leave it on the ferry.'

But the day that had begun foggy and wet – cooler than normal – turned humid by the time he reached the harbor and as the temperature rose so did the smells of Hong Kong, the gritty air and bus fumes, the stewed steam of the mottled seawater sloshing against the ferry pier, the foul dust from the land reclamation, all these stinks clawing at his face. Gray haze became yellow haze and after half an hour – the length of time it took him to reach Hung's neighborhood – the din had worked deep into his ears. Street noise tumbled inside his head.

Crossing Waterloo Road he saw a Union Jack flying over the police station at the corner of Argyle Street. He smiled at it, as though at a circus pennant. Even now the flag seemed like an anachronism, and it was a foreboding of his own imminent departure. When it was gone, would the big red Chinese flag be run up the pole, or would it be the Hong Kong flag with the bauhenia blossom on it – 'A bright, sterile hybrid,' Monty called the colony's flower.

As he glanced up at the flag again he felt a rush of anger. He didn't want the likes of Mr Hung pulling the Union Jack down. The indignity of it! He would lower it slowly himself, and fold it carefully like a napkin, and would tuck it into his suitcase when he left.

On the police station notice board, lettered in large print on three placards, one to a window, were signs reading WANTED PERSON and POLICE REWARD NOTICE and MISSING PERSON. The last one was the category that Mei-ping must have meant when she had said, 'They will put it into the window.' But POLICE REWARD NOTICE was the one that caught his eye, because in addition to the reward – sums up to $100,000 were offered – the crimes were described in precise detail. They were peculiarly Hong Kong crimes – desperate, cruel, often comic, sometimes meaningless. He was reminded of the disfigured woman, and *Your face belongs to me ... I will take your face away.*

In one he read of an army officer who had returned to his office at a certain time to pick up his briefcase and on opening it had been blown up by a bomb that had been slipped into it. A Gurkha soldier was wanted for questioning. Fifty thousand dollars was offered for information leading to the conviction of the person or persons responsible.

Another was recent: *At about 7:50 a.m. on 13 January, 1996, a woman, Miss Cheung Yee Chan was attacked on the 3rd floor balcony of her apartment house on Lai Chi Kok Street, while taking her small child to school. The child was also slashed. Miss Cheung fainted. When she woke she saw her gold jewelry was gone and her child bleeding. He was taken to hospital where he later died. Anyone with information should contact . . .*

Sad, violent, unexplained: was Ah Fu a candidate for the stories in these windows? Trying to imagine her in the list under the heading MISSING PERSON he saw *Woo, Francis Mau Yung*, and thought of his own Mr Woo. This missing person was conceivably his own janitor, Frank Woo, who had not shown up at work for days. He scribbled *Mau Yung* on the back of one of his business cards; he would ask Miss Liu if that was Woo's full name.

He walked on to Hung's apartment house, but still slowly, because he did not know where to begin. It was no help to him to notice that Hung's building was on Waterloo Road while it ran absolutely straight north–south before it twisted past Argyle and Fat Kwong. It seemed no more than a coincidence that Hung's building lay in perfect alignment with Bunt's own building. He derived what he knew was pointless satisfaction seeing, framed by Hung's stair-well window, in a canyon lined with buildings and stuck-out bamboo poles of drying laundry, the old-fashioned tower of Imperial Stitching.

On the fourth-floor landing, Bunt tapped Hung's telephone number into his cellular phone.

'*Wei!*' Hung snarled, sounding surprised and irritable.

'It's me – Neville Mullard.'

'How wonderful to hear your voice.'

Bunt hated him for recovering so quickly.

'Cheers,' Bunt said, at a loss for words.

'Where are you?'

'I am on the landing outside your door,' Bunt said, smiling at the fold-out flap of the phone's mouthpiece.

Hung had fallen silent, and in that silence Bunt rapped hard on the door to the apartment.

Looking naked and slug-like and ambushed, Hung seemed surprised as he answered the door, peering out. He wore baggy pajama bottoms of a sort that made Bunt avert his eyes. Hung's undershirt was frayed and his plastic sandals were as worn and cracked as Wang's – Bunt heard them scuffing to the door. Hung was the picture of a Chinese man interrupted at home: mean, frowsty, damp, rumpled, dozy, like someone tipped out of bed.

'Yah?'

Even his English had become scruffy.

The way Hung opened the door slowly and kept it creaking, checking it when it was the width of his skinny head, suggested he might have been expecting trouble. He seemed anxious, his fingers gripping the door, his yellow fingernails pressed against it as he held it like a shield.

It had bothered Bunt from the first moment of their meeting that Hung was taller than he. He imagined it to be a fraction but it was perhaps as much as an inch. That seemed unnatural, wrong anyway, as Wang's height also seemed wrong, because the Chinese were supposed to be small. Today it bothered Bunt again, because he could not see past Hung to the interior of the room.

'Have you forgotten something?' Hung asked, finding his proper voice.

'I happened to be passing by. I thought we might talk.'

'If only you had called.'

'I jolly well did call,' Bunt said, and waved his cellular phone.

'This is not a convenient time,' Mr Hung said.

The Chinese newspaper in Hung's free hand showed a photograph of a Chinese official wearing an insincere smile and standing next to the Governor-General of Hong Kong. The flashbulb dazzling the lenses of the official's glasses blanked out his eyes. It was a frightening picture. Somewhere in the room behind Hung a television was on; quacky voices and cartoon music exploded from it – a children's program, the violent and silly comics that were broadcast all day on Hong Kong television.

'I need to see you.'

Hung was startled and unprepared. You could not drop in on them: Bunt knew that. Nothing was more menacing to a Hong Kong Chinese than a sudden knock on the door. Nothing was more menacing to a Hong Kong English person either. No one except Americans ever dropped in. But this was the only way of answering Mei-ping's question.

'I am very busy at the moment,' Hung said. Watching kiddie shows? Reading the newspaper? 'We can meet somewhere.'

'Here is fine.'

'I do not entertain at home.'

'You entertained me the other week,' Bunt said. He remembered it clearly because he had found it odd at the time to have an invitation to the man's home.

'I mean in business matters.'

'This isn't business,' Bunt said, clinging to the argument, going closer to Hung who was still squeezed between the door-frame and the partly opened door. 'It's man to man.'

With a sigh that was almost inaudible, Hung said, 'All right then, come back in an hour.'

Another glimpse of a Union Jack, a stack of cages in which frantic twittering birds leapt from perch to perch, a gaudy shrine with a statue of a crazed red-faced devil goddess and a string of fairy lights – this in a glazed fruit shop where a clerk howled into a cellular phone; the squeals of doomed pigs in a passing truck; a family eating a large meal in the middle of a welding workshop, the dainty white tablecloth thrown over a table-saw; big gleaming passenger jets flying low overhead into Kai Tek – it seemed the whole of Kowloon was on the flight path; all this occupied Bunt's idle hour.

On his return, Bunt found Hung transformed, looking remote and almost unapproachable in his melon-colored suit with the Pierre Cardin label on the sleeve. It was a formal visit now. To signify it, because he had been expecting something like this, Bunt carried a pound of glazed fruit under his arm in a bright red box. He handed it over to Hung on his way in, as though it were a permit to admit him to a sad little ceremony in a foreign country.

The country was China. Entering the room, crossing the threshold, was like crossing a frontier. The apartment, so far as he could tell in his swift first glance, was substantially the same: stark, Chinese. Hung was ushering him to a chair, to keep him captive, but Bunt walked to the window and saw again near a winking Belisha beacon on a zebra crossing the Imperial Stitching building up Waterloo Road, the upper windows, executive offices, Miss Liu's office, Lily's cubicle, the cutting floor, the old finishing room, Mr Chuck's office where the blinds were drawn.

Turning back to smile at Hung – at having frustrated his attempt to seat him – Bunt realized that something was different in the room, but what?

'Please.' Mr Hung shoved a chair at him.

Seated, Bunt keenly felt the difference, something missing at the periphery of his gaze.

'Tea,' Hung said. It was a command. He smiled. He withdrew across the shining floor – the afternoon sun blazed there in the varnish.

Where was the white shaggy carpet that had lain there?

'Notice the flat leaves,' Mr Hung was saying – back so soon and already explaining that this was the rarest tea in China, this batch especially, picked from just a small number of bushes on one hillside outside Hangzhou, and all harvested in the month before the Ching Ming Festival.

'Lovely,' Bunt said, deliberately imitating his mother. 'Thanking you.'

'*Lung ching*,' Hung said.

His bony finger pressed on the pot lid as he poured, and though the nail was a yellow claw the finger was as pale as the porcelain.

'Dragon Well,' Hung said.

'Right you are,' Bunt said.

'Perhaps it sounds familiar.'

'It's all Chinese to me,' Bunt said.

'Oh, yes,' Hung said. '*Lung* is dragon in Mandarin, as *loon* is in Cantonese.'

'I think I knew that.'

'Kowloon. Nine dragons.'

'Makes sense.'

'Tong is –'

'Secret society, like a triad.'

'Where did you hear that?'

'I've lived my whole life here,' Bunt said.

'*Tong* is pond.'

'Tong is no such thing,' Bunt said. 'Tong is the sound a bell makes. Tong is like tongue. Tong is a verb like gather, you can tong logs. Tong is one leg of a pair of tongs – what else?'

'Not English,' Mr Hung said. '*Tong* is pond. Kowloon Tong. Nine Dragons Pond.'

'Oh, I see.'

'Where the dragons drink.'

'Of course.'

Hadn't Mr Mo the *feng-shui* geomancer said something of the kind? Chinese was Chinese. All the words had the same sound, all the people the same face. But avon meant river and a Belisha beacon like the one out the window was named after Leslie Hore-Belisha, the Minister of Transport, and did Hung know that?

'Everything means something,' Bunt said.

Hung stared hard at him as though trying to discern the subtle significance of that statement now.

'Green tea has made us healthy,' Hung said.

The cup in his hand, brimming, he placed on the arm of Bunt's chair. He had spread the tea paraphernalia on the little table and that too, the clutter of it, evoked the room as it had been, as he remembered it, not so bare as this. Bunt drank the tea, saying nothing. He had remembered the white carpet especially, for its whiteness and its shaggy pile – and more, but what?

'May I use your facilities?'

Attempting to mask his annoyance, Hung looked twitchy and unsure, and it was apparent that he hated Bunt's asking to penetrate the apartment again. Yet there was nothing Hung could do.

'It's all your bally tea!' He liked the travesty of his mother's manner as a way of baffling Hung.

No carpet in the bathroom either. He was certain there had been one, white, shaggy, inappropriate. That was odd. They threw nothing away. The lid was still down on the WC to prevent the energy from escaping.

'This tea is brewed with water that has not reached the boil,' Hung said, as Bunt sat again. The man was refilling his cup. 'Eighty degrees Celsius is sufficient, unlike the Indian varieties that need to be steeped and brewed.'

'My Mum says you're well-spoken and that's a fact,' Bunt said. He was raising himself on the chair-seat to look out of the window. 'I can see my building.'

Hung moved his head in a sliding manner, sideways, as though beginning a dance step.

'*Feng-shui*,' he said.

'I know that,' Bunt said. He meant the concept – everyone talked about it, even Mr Chuck, the good *feng-shui* of the

Regent, the bad *feng-shui* of the new Bank of China – its triangular thicket of walls and windows.

Hung's head was still sliding, perhaps to capture Bunt's attention, perhaps to emphasize the point.

'They must move back and forth. No obstruction, good *feng-shui*.'

'They?'

'The *Ch'i* of the elements.'

'Mr Chuck found the site for the factory. He had his reasons, I reckon.' Bunt was going to mention the annual visit of Mr Mo, the geomancer, with his *feng-shui* compass disk and his charts and his calculations; but why bother? He had come here to find out what had happened to Ah Fu. 'The factory's well situated. You know that.'

He reasoned that it was probably why Hung had been so persistent: the *feng-shui*. Imperial Stitching was perfectly sited, in the belly of the dragon.

Challenged, Hung merely tightened his features, as though facing a high wind – the sort of look that came into Miss Liu's face when she adjusted the fan in Bunt's office.

'As for our business arrangement,' Hung said, 'there is nothing more to talk about. The deal is in place. More tea?'

'I want to talk about Ah Fu,' Bunt said, feeling that he was flinging himself upon Mr Hung.

'Before you do,' Hung said smoothly, not reacting to what Bunt had said, 'I would like you to see something.'

In his odd loose-jointed household shuffle – so different from the way he marched outside – he hurried to a sideboard, his feet flopping in his sandals, then knelt and opened a small pair of doors, and hovered, rattling papers. Canted over to get a glimpse, Bunt still could not see what the man was doing. The Chinese sideboard might have been an altar.

A large noiseless clock stood on the sideboard showing the wrong time and it was another intimation that Bunt was in China, where he imagined it was always the wrong time. The hands indicated three-fifteen, but it was now four-thirty. China was late, China was slow and inaccurate and outmoded. It was a mechanical clock, imitation French, on gilt feet, in a sun-faded or perhaps fake wooden case the color of a pumpkin. The roundness of the clock was in marked contrast to Hung's narrow skull.

After closing and latching the doors of the sideboard – no, it had to be an altar – Hung got to his feet and hovered over Bunt, passing him an envelope as though dealing a playing-card.

'For you.'

The red *lai see* packet stamped with gold Chinese characters was familiar to Bunt as the sort of envelope Hong Kong Chinese presented on festivals when they offered gifts of lucky money. Mr Chuck had given him many such envelopes, but always at Christmas and on birthdays. It was more suited to the formality of Hung's apartment, to this whole ritual of unanswered questions.

'Open it, if you please.'

Squeezing it, then blowing it open with a puff of breath, the inflated packet revealed a folded piece of paper which Bunt unfolded. It was a Bank of China check made out to him for fifty thousand dollars. That was forty-five hundred pounds – Hung was still talking.

'And I've already given one to your mother.'

'Thanking you.' She hadn't mentioned it.

But it was a check. A Chinese check like a Chinese everything else was so much an imitation it was probably unusable, just an exercise in mimicry. This was no doubt rubber, and even if it was not it was symbolic money, not negotiable, only a tentative promise that might never be fulfilled. They were all paper-hangers, the Chinese in Hong Kong, check-kiters and price-grubbers and pay-gougers. The check in the red envelope meant nothing to him – even antagonized him, but so that Hung would be placated Bunt made all the appropriate noises.

'Not for Full Moon receiving company,' Hung said, nodding furiously. 'This is a personal gift. A little present between friends. To show gratitude and trust.'

Handing over a chunk of money at an awkward moment was another example of Chinese subtlety. As usual there was no mistaking its purpose: to obligate and encumber Bunt, to distract him – in what?

He was certain that Hung had interrupted him in something but he could not remember precisely what it had been.

Bunt smiled in confusion and then, wildly looking around, he caught sight of the clock and saw that it was still three-fifteen. The hands had not moved. Not slow, it had stopped. And another disturbing detail – the glass was gone from its face, smashed probably, when the clock stopped at that hour. Calculating in this way, Bunt remembered his question.

'Ah Fu seems to be missing.'

'Yes?' Hung's way of showing indifference or denial, Bunt saw, was to hold his hands at the level of his waist and shake his fingers in a twinkling fashion as though drying them.

'Ah Fu hasn't been to work for a week.'

Hung's mask was his expression of facing a high wind, cheeks sucked in, eyes narrowed to slits, giving nothing away. It was the making of poker-faces in which the Chinese were expert and enigmatic.

'So we're wondering,' Bunt said to the unhelpful man.

'Obviously she is feeling poorly. She is home.'

'Her flat-mate hasn't seen her and she's very worried. So am I.'

'And me.'

'Good. Because you were the last person to see her,' Bunt said.

He got up from his chair. Hung side-stepped as though to obstruct him, but Bunt pushed past him and walked the length of the room to the window, looking forth. He saw his building and he was so absorbed in the harmony of straight lines that linked this window with his windows he had to reach to the wall and steady himself on a cabinet.

'Careful,' the Chinese man said, taking a step towards him.

Bunt had snagged his fingers on a shelf, having reached through the cabinet door. There was no glass in the door. The crockery was gone from inside. Fewer knick-knacks cluttered the shelves. A silver spoon, a painted tin cat and a brass bell, that was all. Where was the porcelain? Where was the glass?

He was in China, standing on a dusty carpetless floor, with bare walls, the glass missing from the cabinet door and from the face of the stopped clock. It was strange and spare, a Chinese apartment that was an experience of China.

Hong Kong people seldom entertained at home but when they did they gloated over their appliances and their toys: they were spenders, they hated treasures, they loved gadgets. As refugees they valued portable property most of all, things they could stuff into bags and flee with. But Hung's drab place was what he had always imagined China to be like, fiercely frugal, stinking of cabbage and fried noodles and cheesy feet, where people sat upright in hard chairs in their underwear.

'Ah Fu left the restaurant with you.'

'Did you observe us leaving?'

Bunt hesitated, and before he could think of anything to say Hung was attacking.

'See?' Hung said. 'You are very much mistaken.'

Bunt was on the point of telling him that Mei-ping had seen them leave in a taxi, but he thought better of it. Better to keep her out of it.

'Perhaps Ah Fu visited her family in China.'

'She was afraid of going there. She wanted to emigrate to Canada.'

'That's it then,' Hung said. 'She has left for Canada. She is young. Young people are not always reliable.'

'She worked for me,' Bunt said. 'She was never absent, never late.'

Hung had not stopped smiling, though it was his wind-blown expression, squinting into a gale.

'Who is inquiring about her?'

'I am.'

'But you said "we're wondering."'

Bunt stared at him.

'Please sit down,' Hung said.

Instead of doing so, Bunt put his hands on his hips and said, 'If she's missing, it's a matter for the police.'

'That is not a good idea,' Hung said. 'The police would simply make trouble.'

It annoyed Bunt to hear Hung say the very words he himself had said to Mei-ping.

'Trouble for you.'

'Trouble for us.'

'Something might have happened to Ah Fu,' Bunt said, and took a step closer to Hung, who did not move.

Hung said, 'In the course of a police inquiry they would look into your business. Your records and mine. They would discover that we have started a new company in the Cayman Islands and that money was being transferred in a manner that was highly questionable. You see?'

But Bunt was already protesting. 'I don't have to sell to you!'

Still talking calmly Hung said, 'And your mother might find that dreadfully inconvenient.'

Bunt was silenced, he hated that tone, its arrogant presumption, hated it most because he was sure that Hung was right. His mother's Chinese nature said, *Don't get involved*.

The way in which Hung had peeled the chicken feet and picked out the stringy tendons and gnawed at the yellow shanks; the slant of his lips as he stuffed his mouth with chicken breast and spoke of trussing the birds with string; and *I want to eat your foot*, and the tantrum over the bitter melon; and the abruptness with which he had poked a piece of cheap jade into Ah Fu's mouth – it all came back to Bunt as he faced Hung, and the logic in it was like a warning prelude to a violent crime.

You would see all these images on a Chinese scroll and you would know without seeing the corpse that a murder had been committed.

'Your mother would want you to mind your own business.'

Bunt saw it clearly: the glass had been smashed in the struggle, the clock flung to the floor, the cabinet tipped over, the carpets rucked up. And when Ah Fu became desperate Hung had lashed out and hurt her – cracked her skull perhaps – and she had bled all over the white shag carpets. The evidence was not in the room, the evidence was missing – that stark neatness was the proof that a bloody crime had been committed. The same was true of China. The look of the apartment was the spare look of China, a place that had been scoured and simplified by chaos – upheaval, terror, mass murder, war. Hong Kong had a peaceable clutter, just an accumulation of worn or out-of-date things, like a massive attic.

'Someone will ask,' Bunt said.

'Only a busybody.'

'Plenty of them in Hong Kong. It's not China, you know.'

'Ah Fu is where she wants to be.' Hung stared a moment longer. 'It is wrong to interfere in people's private affairs.'

'If a person's dead of natural causes it's private,' Bunt said. 'If she's been killed it's everyone's business.'

'I think your mother would disagree.'

With the sudden adroitness with which he had offered Bunt tea at an awkward moment, Hung said, 'Do you remember that I told you that Wendell in the Pussy Cat is a Eurasian?'

'Yes,' Bunt said, surprised by the obliqueness of the question.

'Wonderful. Wendell is your brother. Half-brother, I should say.'

'That's a lie!'

Bunt had backed to the door, where he heard a radio – Cantonese gabbling, loud music, the sound of phones ringing and traffic toiling in the busy road below. How dare Hung say that to him?

Yes, Hong Kong was harmless clutter, but the Chinese were brutes and China in Bunt's imagining looked spare because so much had been broken. All the crockery in China had been smashed – flung over the years in all the periodic convulsions for which China was famous. All the blood-stained carpets had been tossed away. All the ancestors' portraits had been destroyed. All the bodies had been buried. It was a country of bare rooms and empty shelves, like this apartment.

'Someone might go to the police.'

'That would be a mistake.'

Bunt said nothing. He was glad to go.

ELEVEN

When he got home from Hung's and did not see his mother anywhere in the cottage he thought she might be dead.

So many years of unvarying routine made the slightest change a shock for Bunt. He was uneasy without a program; he could not improvise. He counted on morning tea brought on a tray by Wang at six, on breakfast itself at seven, the tram or the car at eight, arriving in Kowloon Tong at nine, coffee and biscuits at eleven, lunch at one, tea at four, the Pussy Cat at five-thirty, Cricket Club on Wednesday, Mei-ping for sex, his mother always waiting for him.

'Don't you get fed up when everything's the same?' Mr Chuck had once said to him.

'I'd be terrified if it weren't.'

Perhaps that had influenced the old man's decision to bequeath his share of Imperial to Bunt. It was Mr Chuck's fault that lately – since his death – so much had changed. All the funeral arrangements, and the business with Monty; his sole ownership of Imperial Stitching; Hung.

Wang had become ever more silent. He jogged more, as though punishing himself – Bunt saw him hobbling up the Peak Road. Jogging was one of those outdoor activities that told everything about the person doing it. When he had given up smoking Bunt had been told to try it, and so he had scrutinized the punished-looking people going up and down the Peak. Jogging was a frenzied dance of revelation – goggling eyes, hollow cheeks, blush patches on thighs and arms, wobbly joints. They always looked on the point of surrender. All the jogger's ill-health and anxiety showed in the odd slow hopping. Anyone could see that Wang was suffering.

Meals were not always on time. Bunt was frequently late. The deal with Mr Hung seemed to have improved his mother's tastes. She had begun to have a pair of kippers with breakfast, and smoked salmon instead of paste sandwiches with her tea. And now the disappearance of Ah Fu. Chaos.

'Mum?'

The fear in his own voice frightened him. Bunt looked around the empty house, turning on lights with his face averted, as though he expected to see his mother's body on the floor. To impose order, to claim his house, he made a pot of tea and sat with it, wringing his hands, disturbed by his memory of the visit to Hung's. Mei-ping would ask him about it. He thought of calling her – no, it was better, simpler to explain it to her in person. That was another change in his life: he had begun to want to see her – not only for sex, he needed her in a different way. He wished he had good news for her.

Then, aware that he was thinking of Mei-ping at the moment his mother might be dead, he was ashamed and remorseful, and he guiltily blamed Mei-ping for his distraction.

A moment later he heard a car in the lane, saw from the window it was a taxi, and then his mother was hurrying into the house, laughing like a drain.

'Where have you been?'

It hardly mattered because here she was, breathless and happy, looking slightly tipsy, yet he was angry with her for having frightened him and he wanted to scold. He knew he sounded like her on a bad night.

'Having a flutter.'

'I was worried sick. I thought something terrible had happened.'

'Don't be such a nancy. "Something terrible."'

'People disappear, you know,' he said. A catch in his throat prevented him from saying more for a moment. 'What sort of flutter?'

'How many sorts are there, Bunt? Use your loaf.'

'There's all sorts of punters, Mum, and you know it.'

He was trembling. He seemed furious, taking issue with her in her sloppy logic, but his anger was all fueled by the fear that she might have been dead.

'Now that you mention it, I suppose so,' she said. But she was indifferent, still smiling. 'I was at Happy Valley, wasn't I?'

He had so many clear memories of all their confidences at Happy Valley that just the mention of the place helped to ease his mood. Yet he had never known her to gamble in the middle of a week and certainly not to talk about it in this way. She seemed to be boasting.

'You won,' he said. He did not say more, he did not even phrase what was in his mind, but his partially formed thought was in the nature of, *When has she ever lost?*

'Told you I had a bit of luck, didn't I?'

Another wide smile rearranged her face, drew up the bags of her cheeks, distorted her features like surgery, made her squint like a goblin.

Never mind the boldness in gambling large sums – they must have been, otherwise (normally a timid punter) she would not have made such a meal of it. Where had she got the money from?

Then he remembered, *And I've already given one to your*

mother – the fifty thousand Hong Kong dollars. So the check Hung had given her as a sweetener she had already cashed, and had used it betting on the horses.

'And I might hare off to Sha Tin tomorrow if the going is good.'

Mei-ping was waiting for him at his office door. Her face was set in a stare of interrogation. Sometimes she had no eyes, or they were small and dark and teasing; but this morning they were lit with serious concern and they penetrated to his heart. She wanted answers.

Trying to brush past her, Bunt said, 'I've got some paperwork to attend to.'

He had nothing but fear. He wanted to hide. Yet she believed his lie.

'Miss Liu?' he called out, and as soon as he spoke her name he heard Miss Liu's chair being kicked back and saw the woman herself was at the door. His old horror of improvisation made his mind go blank, but in his panic – thrashing about for something to say – he remembered talking to her about the flag, and her saying that Mr Woo had not shown up, and this brought forth the sight of Mr Woo's name among the missing persons in the list posted in the police station window.

'Mr Woo – is he still off work?'

'Still off.'

'What is Mr Woo's name?'

'Name Frank.'

'His full name, including his Chinese name, Miss Liu, if you please.'

'I will just check up.'

He noticed that Mei-ping had not moved. 'You see how busy I am?'

Mei-ping lowered her eyes, but she stood her ground. The

Chinese were not confrontational, they did not have a lot to say, but they could be stubborn.

'I've got so much on my plate,' Bunt said. 'My mother's gambling again.'

He tried to make it sound like a serious affliction.

'Did you see Mr Hung?'

It saddened him that no matter how contemptuous she was of the man, hating his bullying manner, and even suspecting him of murder, still she went on calling him mister. But that was perhaps an important thing about the Chinese, their ability to render certain words meaningless.

'I saw him yesterday. I went to his flat,' Bunt said. 'That's what I want to tell you about, when I have a free moment.'

She peered at him as though trying to see hope in his eyes, any promise, anything bright, leaning slightly like someone at a fence, looking harder and deeper.

'It's going to be all right,' Bunt said.

But he was not thinking of the flat at all, or of Hung. Having seen the flat, the significant changes, he had the gloomiest forebodings about the fate of Ah Fu. He could not say this to Mei-ping at the moment, but he was thinking: *Ah Fu may be gone, but never mind – you've got me. And perhaps Ah Fu has not gone.*

Miss Liu put her head out the door and said, 'Francis Mau Yung Woo.'

No, Ah Fu was gone.

'What is the matter?' Mei-ping said, seeing his face change.

'Nothing,' he said, but thought: *Everything*. And for the first time after hearing the shocking assertion, he believed there might be some truth in what Hung had said about the barman Wendell in the Pussy Cat being his half-brother.

Mei-ping believed the worst about Ah Fu, he could tell it as she was leaving to go back to work, from the angle of her small shoulders.

Instead of having lunch at his desk he went to the Pussy Cat and hid, drinking a beer and trying to read the *South China Morning Post*. Nearly the entire front page was devoted to the Chinese Take-away. He drank some more and seeing a large photograph of a lovely fox-faced woman he looked for information about her in the caption – perhaps her name, her nationality, some clue to why he liked looking at her face – and read, *There is no beauty that hath not some strangeness in the proportion.*

'What's that all about!' he said, suddenly cross for having been thwarted – all he wanted to know was the woman's name.

He threw the paper down, and sat against the side of the booth letting the loud music deafen him and concentrating on the dancers. It was another example of his growing sense of chaos. He had sometimes gone to the Pussy Cat in the middle of the working day, but when had he sat watching the topless Filipinos without any intention of leaving?

He craned his neck to get a glimpse in the bar mirror of Wendell, who was frowning at the races on television.

'You look just like your father,' the Mamasan said.

Hearing that, his sense of desolation was complete.

One of the dancers, he saw, was Baby. She was dancing badly, smiling in the mirror, unsteady in her high heels. She had a lovely body, full breasts and slender legs and a soft puppy-like face that made her seem simple and credulous. It also reminded Bunt of her on all fours on the carpet of the blue hotel smiling back at him and saying, *Let we make some fuppies.*

After the music stopped she joined him, now wearing a dress. 'You like my new dress?' she asked. 'It is my best color.'

It was too dark in the booth for Bunt to be able to see it.

He touched the silky cloth – it was a Chinese synthetic – and said, 'What color?'

'Furple.'

'Of course,' he said. He was still holding the soft sleeve of the dress, reflecting on its origin. 'What are you going to do next year when the Chinese take over?'

'Maybe we Filipinos just go away, back home.'

When he said 'you' she understood this to mean every Filipino person in Hong Kong.

'You like it there?'

'Of course I hate it.' She had a wonderful toothy smile. 'The Peelipeens is shit.'

'Why do you say that?'

He found this so restful, drinking beer in the middle of the day in a darkened bar, talking nonsense to an uncritical listener.

'Because it is my home,' Baby said. 'But other people they like it. Foreigners like it. You will like it.'

'I'd like to go there.'

He considered this in an idle way, inventing a life, hypothesizing his moves, from arriving there and meeting someone like Baby, to raising children and perhaps starting a business. He got that far and then became obscurely anxious – was it the children or was it everything he had heard about the Philippines, the danger and dog-eating and disorder? All he could imagine with any conviction was sitting in a bar in Manila doing what he was doing now, drinking beer and talking nonsense to a pretty girl.

'Come to Manila,' Baby said. 'I will be you wipe.'

'I'm crazy,' Bunt said. He knew he was not crazy. He felt he might be difficult. 'You don't want me.'

'Nobody be perpeck,' Baby said. 'I like crazy. My friends are crazy.'

Bunt said nothing. She seemed friendly and forgiving but

she was ridiculous and she was making him ridiculous. He did not know why he was hiding from Mei-ping, but it helped to be here – now at least. Tormenting him with her silliness, Baby made him think only of the virtues of Mei-ping.

'You staying here next year?'

'I don't know,' Bunt said.

'My Mummy knows the Chinese,' Baby said.

'My Mum does as well!'

Bunt knew that Baby's mother was a cleaner at a Chinese home in Mid-Levels. Her sister was a nurse's helper in a madhouse in Chai Wan. Baby herself, when she was not dancing topless, worked in a posh hotel as a cleaner and had many stories of being propositioned by guests, both men and women. They lived together in a tiny room in Kennedy Town. The first time he had met Baby, in Jack's Place, she claimed she was Spanish.

'Chinese people keep you in a room, and men go in and abuse you and have sex with you. If you cry, never mind, they like to hear it. Don't laugh or they hit you harder. Then the Chinese people lock you up again.'

It sounded like the voice of experience, but the ringing in Bunt's ears told him he was drunk.

'They won't put me in a room,' he said. 'Tell me about Manila.'

'My Daddy have a junk shop in Manila,' she said.

'That's enough,' he said. 'Don't tell me anything more.'

By mid-afternoon, leaving the Pussy Cat, Bunt had just about decided that he wanted to marry Mei-ping. All the time with Baby had helped him make up his mind. He was always too confused in Mei-ping's presence to reach any conclusions, and often with Mei-ping he thought of Baby, of her willingness to consider any of his suggestions; the penalty was that then he, Bunt, had to consider anything she suggested, and nearly always she asked for money, or a favor, for her sister or mother – air-tickets, clothes, jewelry, and on one occasion a television set. Or the ultimate condition, *I let you do it to me all the time when we get to England* . . . Sitting with Baby in the Pussy Cat, the loud music battering his head, drinking expensive bottles of beer, he found it easy to settle on Mei-ping. Drinking in the bar with Baby had made him amorous for Mei-ping. It was often that way with him – the presence of one woman made him desire the company of another. But this was desire of a different kind. Because it encompassed something more than sex – he imagined himself wanting to hang around after sex and not go back to his mother – he thought of it as love.

He had been dreading going back to England with his mother. Living with Mei-ping would make England easier to bear – he would be carrying a bit of Hong Kong back with him, the best bit, and also the most portable. It was like the fantasy he and Corkill had developed in the school yard, of the insatiable Chinese mistress in the manor house, her red nails, her slinky nightdress, her pretty knickers. That was a schoolboy's fantasy, but there was enough of his own yearning in it to stir him still.

Marrying was a gamble but it was less of a gamble now that he had money. Nor was he choosing to leave Hong Kong: he was being sent away by Hung. And he felt distanced from his mother – the deal with Hung had proved to him how different he was from his mother. He would never have sold his three-quarters share of the factory had it not been for her insistence, her saying there was no future here. His mother had made him listen to Hung. The damned woman had conspired with Hung, and what for?

The risk in marrying Mei-ping was not the same risk as a wager at Sha Tin, where it was win or lose. In marriage there would be some happiness. He would ask Monty to prepare a pre-nuptial agreement, so that he would not be gutted in the event of a divorce. If it didn't work they would go their separate ways. But he felt he would never stop loving her, and what convinced him was that he needed her in a way that transcended sex. He wanted to carry her to England to be his wife, by his side, until he died.

He asked Miss Liu to find Mei-ping as soon as he got back to his office.

'What's wrong?' he asked her, when they were alone, she on his sofa, Bunt at his desk.

'I had my nightmare,' she said.

She was gaunt and attractive, and haunted in a way that made Bunt want again to hold her, to possess her, and to stay with her, lying next to her instead of going home. When she had seemed strong, saying 'Do you want me?', he had demanded that she make love to him while, abstracted, he looked down at her busying herself with his body.

Now, pale, thin, with the large eyes of hunger or illness shining in her bony face, twisting her hands, slightly stooped, her pain apparent in her shoulders, Mei-ping seemed almost to glow, the way the skin of sick people is often illuminated with a pale bluish light. It made him feel powerful and dominant, urging her to lie back and part her legs, and he could just imagine her closing her eyes and smiling with pleasure as he entered her and roused her and gave her some of his strength.

'Please,' she said, because he was trying to hold her hand.

He had kicked the office door shut. Miss Liu was typing. Mr Cheung's chair creaked in his cubicle. He could hear cartons being thrown onto trucks in the loading bay at Shipping. In Stitching the machines were rattling and every so often he could hear the bite of the guillotine in Cutting.

It did not seem to him that he was drunk, although he had been with Baby for several hours in the Pussy Cat. Yet the way that Mei-ping fended off his advances suggested that she thought he was drunk – that he needed to be fended off, that he would not notice.

'I want to explain Mr Hung,' he said. He crossed the office and sat next to her on the sofa, as though he was being solicitous. His brain was turning very slowly. But she had not asked anything about Hung. He held a conversation with himself in this silence, reasoning with himself, and remembering. At the end of it he said, 'Did you say nightmare?'

She tried to give him his damp hand back and when he refused it, she placed it in his lap, as though dropping a crab into a basket.

'I have the nightmare all the time,' she said. 'It is of Happy Valley. Someone is being punished.'

'Punished how?'

'Punished the Chinese way. They have led the person onto the racecourse blindfolded. The stands are full of people – Chinese people – but there is no race. No horses, no happiness. It is just Chinese men in uniforms on the big TV screen. I see the person kneeling.'

Bunt was nodding, and his hand like the crab it had seemed crept crab-wise out of his lap towards Mei-ping's thigh.

'Last night the person was Ah Fu.'

With that, Bunt's hand went dead. He said, 'That's what I meant to talk to you about.'

'The soldiers walked behind her and shot her in the back of the neck and all the people in Happy Valley were clapping their hands,' Mei-ping said. 'That is the Chinese way.'

It was horrible to him: he could see it clearly, the TV screen, the crowds in the stands, the banners, the red flags, the kneeling Ah Fu and the execution on the green grass at the center of the racecourse.

The idea that Mei-ping had this horrific vision late at night, alone, crouched on her narrow bed in her room in

Lai Chi Kok filled him with pity, and he desired her again. His fingers lifted and he touched her hand.

Mei-ping shrank and folded her arms and she tucked away the hand he had touched. Then she moved down the sofa from him, once again seeming to fend him off, and said, 'What did Mr Hung tell you about Ah Fu?'

'Only that he hadn't seen her.'

'Mr Hung is lying.' Mei-ping became sorrowful. 'I thought maybe she is at his flat. You didn't see her there?'

'No.'

He knew he sounded unconvincing. It was the effect of suppressing so much of what he had noticed: the missing carpets, the pane of glass missing in the cabinet, the porcelain missing from the shelves, the stopped clock with the smashed face.

'Ah Fu is in trouble,' Mei-ping said. 'The police will know.'

Bunt said, 'Listen. If there's been a crime it will do no good to go to the police. That will just make it worse for everyone.'

'Not worse for Ah Fu.'

Her simplicity made her clear-sighted. This was unanswerable. Bunt could not think of anything to say.

'They will find the person who did it,' she said.

'Maybe they'll suspect you. You're the last person who saw her.'

'Mr Hung was the last person.'

'Yes, but he'll tell whoppers. Suspicion will fall on you. Don't you see?'

Though he had not rehearsed this and hardly believed it, saying it to her and watching her react with fear made it seem plausible.

'I am innocent,' Mei-ping said.

'Of course,' Bunt said, and now he took a deep breath,

for he was about to deliver the lines he had rehearsed. 'But listen. Perhaps she is gone. Perhaps something went wrong. Perhaps Mr Hung is responsible. But you have me.'

In his rehearsal he had seen her smile through her tears as he said this, and she fell into his arms. But instead her face crumpled and she began to cry bitterly as she had yesterday holding the scissors. He watched her, desiring her again, wanting to embrace her.

He lifted his arms but before he could seize her and save her, she got up quickly, inefficiently – she was not well – and hurried from the room.

He hoped that no one had witnessed her leaving his office in tears, and so as not to call attention to her leaving he waited several minutes, and then strolled – forced himself to stroll – to the elevator, to her floor, to her work station.

The other girls wearing their safety bonnets to keep their hair out of their work, away from the spinning fly-wheels of their machines, were bent over scraps of cloth. One stool was empty. He saw a girl giggling at him, astonished to see the boss there for the second time that day.

'Mei-ping?'

'Gone.'

He pretended not to care. He smiled at the stool. He sauntered to the door and shut it carefully. And then he stumbled down the stairs and dashed as fast as he could to Kowloon Tong Police Station, where he imagined that Mei-ping was spilling her guts, and he guided himself by using the Union Jack on the rooftop flag-pole, lifting in a freshening wind – the sort of sudden sea-breeze that often meant rain.

He was proud of the place. Here, Hong Kong was not a frenzy of marketeers and plonkers yattering on cellular phones; it was the rule of law, it was decorum and order. It was the solid building with its serious entrances and its scowling windows, all bars and screens, the dark uniforms, the black boots, the swept floor, the row of chairs, another flag inside, and the portrait of the Queen that was hung on the wall beside the sergeant at the desk.

'Yes?' the sergeant said, glancing up from a log-book.

'I was looking for someone.'

'You want to report a missing person?'

'Not at all, just looking for a friend who said she might be stopping by.'

He knew as soon as he said that it was wrong to use the expression 'stopping by,' for why would anyone stop by a police station, especially the forbidding one in Kowloon Tong?

'Her cat's missing. Sort of brown stripes.'

Because he was usually truthful he was an inept liar – unimaginative, unconvincing, careless, worst of all he always gave too much information. Brown stripes was a mistake.

'We don't find missing cats.'

'She thought it might be stolen. You deal with theft, don't you?'

'Stolen cat,' the sergeant said. It was all he needed to say in order to mock Bunt's confusion. He returned to his log book muttering in Cantonese.

It was raining when Bunt left the police station. His mother said she liked the rain – it always reminded her of Uncle Ron's bungalow in Worthing on a wet Sunday; but his mother was thinking of a downpour on her small corner of the Peak, with the roof of the Fire Station gleaming on the bluff just below. That was atmospheric rain. In Kowloon Tong the rain came down like a curse, the thunder slipping between the buildings and tearing at the laundry on the stuck-out poles and battering the awnings of the stall-holders. It went on falling, whitening the mildew on the housing blocks, and snarling traffic, and speeding the pedestrians – making them push each other – and sloshing into the dirty gutters like Chinese stew.

He stepped backwards into a doorway where a young man seemed to be coughing and spitting into a cellular phone. No: Bunt smiled, proud of his mistake – the man was speaking in his own language and Bunt invented the idea that it was an affectionate monologue, the gagging man, his face contorted, his teeth covered in spittle, biting on the mouthpiece of the receiver in a doorway in Kowloon Tong as the rain came down.

He was disgusted by the repulsive man for suggesting the idea to him, but he took out his own cellular phone and called Mei-ping, for if she was not at the police station reporting Ah Fu's disappearance, what was she doing?

At ten rings he was going to hang up, but it was still raining, he was in the doorway, he had nothing else to do, and the repetition of the rings began to calm his spirits with their monotony. It rang on, a dozen more times, and at last he was so surprised when the ringing stopped that he almost hung up. A timid voice detained him.

'Yes?'

Though the voice was small it was filled with shock and fear, like the piercing cry of an insect.

'It's me,' he said.

'Please come.'

'When?'

'Now, please.'

His heart swelled with joy. 'Right you are,' he said to the sudden hum of the dial tone, for Mei-ping had rung off.

In all the time he had known Mei-ping – the seven years she had worked at Imperial Stitching – he had only been to her building once and never to her flat. The place was on the western edge of Lai Chi Kok near the noisy land reclamation which threw up dust and looked like a desert. The single time he had been there was after a Christmas party. Mei-ping had not asked him in, so she said, because Ah Fu was there. It was awkward, even shameful for her to turn up with her drunken gweilo boss.

Today she had invited him and he was thrilled. Seeing Bunt getting out of a taxi, a small Chinese child burst into tears at this fearful apparition of the balding devil and ran to clutch his mother's legs to cower in terror. The woman laughed loudly in embarrassment.

Bunt looked up and saw Mei-ping's face peering down at him from a third-floor balcony. He ran up a littered stair well to where she waited, hugging herself with her skinny arms.

She seemed strangely at home here, almost anonymous, but Bunt knew that the anxiety that turned her weak and pale and luminous had made her look like the rest of the inhabitants of Lai Chi Kok. She said nothing to him. She walked away abruptly, meaning it as a signal that he must follow her.

She pushed the door of her flat open. She stood aside. She said, 'Look.'

Though Bunt had never seen the flat before, he knew at once that something was wrong. It was lopsided, it was gappy, drawers were pulled out and they sagged, but they were empty. One entire side of the room was bare, but from the patches of dust and the sun-faded portions on the walls he knew that the bare side had once been furnished, perhaps even cluttered. A closet-door was ajar – that closet too was half empty.

'What's missing?'

'Everything of Ah Fu.'

It was gone, every trace of Ah Fu, all she had owned.

'My poor darling,' he said.

He embraced Mei-ping, and it took most of his self-control to be gentle and not to squeeze the life out of her. Yet she did not resist. She accepted his hands. He felt her skeleton in his fingers. He was aroused, excited, panting with anticipation, his blood throbbing against his eyes. He wanted to kiss her. That she did resist.

'I must go away from here,' she said. 'I am afraid.'

TWELVE

To calm her, to calm himself, Bunt – who had never been so rash – took a chance and said, 'Let's go to Macao.'

Saying it he gagged a little, because it seemed such a risky plunge into the unknown.

Mei-ping said, 'Okay,' and he almost suffocated. Then he told himself that she wanted to be with him and that it was Friday and he began to breathe in more regular gulps.

What he had felt had no name he could think of, yet the obscure lowness of spirit reminded him of his mood after a dismal day in Kowloon Tong when he knew his mother was waiting for him on the Peak. He needed to be consoled against a woman's breasts.

Mei-ping no longer seemed like a strange Chinese woman with a Chinese problem. She was like him, she resembled him, her hunger was his hunger and her answer to that hunger was his too. She was part of him, the rest of him. He looked at her and saw himself – not his face but one of his limbs. He wondered if he might be in love, but it was a word he never used, like cancer or joy, so he could only make a stab at its meaning.

The fugitive gleam in Mei-ping's eyes gave her a pained yearning gaze. She seemed to be staring at something so private, so distant, he could not see it. He knew that she felt insecure, that she was taking a gamble too, that she was fearful, perhaps desperate.

'Maybe Ah Fu came back and picked up her stuff.'

'No,' Mei-ping said, still staring; and again, 'no.'

Every other possibility was ominous, and if it was Mr Hung who had done it, what next?

Bunt tried to hold Mei-ping's hand, but it was so hard for him to grip its limpness, to press reassurance into something that was so yielding and passive. Her hand was a small blind boneless creature he needed to protect.

He told himself that she was stunned at the moment but that when she got over it she would realize that he was rescuing her and would be grateful. He was aroused by her, he loved having her so near him in the ordinariness of the crowd of somber pedestrians, but he also knew that what he wanted from her now would not be satisfied by an hour in a blue hotel.

Sex was something related to this feeling, but sex was simpler, sex had an end, a sudden finish, a squirt and then a stumble, leaving him with a damp amnesia that puzzled him and made him stupid. He always lay there afterwards as slack as a fish on a slab, feeling sticky, his body reeking of fish. And after sex you got out of bed and went home. But this was different. He wanted more. He could not imagine being free of the feeling.

'Have you ever been in love?' he asked.

'I don't know.'

'You must have loved someone.'

'I love Ah Fu,' she said.

She began to cry in her suffering way, reluctantly sobbing, stony-faced, trying to stop herself as the tears ran down her cheeks.

He could not reply: in his love for Mei-ping he had almost forgotten Ah Fu.

Silent in the taxi, silent in the Star Ferry, and in the short walk to the terminal stairway; silent in the embarkation line, silent in the jet-foil to Macao.

The last time he had been this way was with Baby on a Saturday night two years before, goatishly snorting with anticipation on the run over. He had bought her a new dress for the occasion. She sat with her knees together smoothing it, as he pinched her like a monkey. She encouraged him by giggling and telling him insincerely to stop it. Heading for a hotel called the Pagoda she saw a photo studio and said she wanted a photograph taken showing them together. It was developed while they waited, and Bunt felt they looked such a ridiculous couple that his ardor ebbed.

But the room at the Pagoda was so viciously dirty and so dimly lit that he was aroused again. Baby knew it. She got down on her hands and knees and said 'Woof! Woof!' and laughed as he mounted her, clutching her smooth waist. But when it was over – minutes later – he wanted to go back to Hong Kong. He felt bruised and miserable, and he lay like a fish, inventing excuses. *I've just remembered* . . . He canceled the rest of the stay, the overnight. Baby did not seem to mind, and he was relieved to have her permission to go back to his mother – thankful to her for releasing him. When she said, 'I need some money,' he gladly handed it over. And there was the disastrous night with Rosa Rabbit, the hairy Coelho woman.

This was different, this was headlong and desperate. A man sitting next to Mei-ping in the jet-foil was wolfing a paper cup of soupy noodles, and they could see nothing through the port-holes except the rusty hulls of ships in the Hong Kong harbor roads and, in the channel, the dim shadows of coasts – Lantau must have been one, Cheung Chau another; and the ambiguous stripe formed by the gray sea meeting the gray sky might have been China. But what did it matter? In the monotony of all this Bunt felt such joy in being with Mei-ping that he imagined that this was how gamblers must feel when they wagered their whole fortune on a single number on the turn of a card, and won.

This is what winning is like, he thought. The jet-foil was full of gamblers – it had to be on a Friday night. He was delighted to be one of them. The jackpot was already his. He was going to Macao not to gamble but to collect his winnings.

Night fell as the growling vessel lost power and settled into the water and moved slowly toward the pier at Macao. The lights of the city dotting the slopes of a hill lay reflected in bright misshapen puddles in the harbor. Mei-ping had not spoken; she did not speak now; she was anxious and moved stiffly, as though thinking of something else. She did not respond when Bunt touched her and so he left her alone but stayed near her, like a house-boy or a husband – or like a son, for that was how he handled his mother, keeping out of her way but remaining alert. He liked the role of helper and though Mei-ping did not understand what he was doing now she would eventually realize how useful he was; that he might be indispensable.

For part of the way in the jet-foil, Bunt had imagined arriving in London with Mei-ping: having her on his arm, buying her meals, showing her the sights. So engrossed was he that he could not see himself in London without her. Loving her, having her, meant that he would be able to go back. In the country house that somewhat resembled the country house of his and Corkill's fantasy he stood at the window with Mei-ping, and perhaps she was wearing a diaphanous dress and high heels, and cows were grazing in a nearby meadow. 'Holsteins,' he heard himself saying. 'And that is the bull – watch what he does.'

There were long lines at Macao Immigration – and the signs in Portuguese made him think of Europe in a way that English signs in Hong Kong never did. The passengers shuffled between stanchions and fences towards the desks of immigration officials. Bunt and Mei-ping were divided by the signs *Hong Kong Citizens* and *Other Countries*. They met on the far side of the barrier, still saying nothing; and then were in another taxi.

What Bunt could see of Macao from the taxi window was the same hill he had seen from the pier, and another escarpment of winking lights, casinos on cliffs, casinos on boulevards, casinos bulking all over the promenade. That was the twilit city, yet night had already cast its shadow over the distant hills, and that shadow was Chinese.

They had no luggage. Bunt considered this: no clothes, no spongebags, no cases. But that act of sudden flight, dropping everything and catching the jet-foil, pleased him. He had never taken such a gamble. He had never won so much. Speeding on the smooth road around the harbor curve the taxi tipped Mei-ping's slender body against him with such pressure he could sense the heat through her dress.

'The Bela Vista,' he said to the driver.

'Yes, yes.'

But he had repeated it because surely the man spoke Portuguese and little English, and he wanted to be sure. It was the only good hotel he knew. He did not want to go near the Pagoda with its memories of 'Woof! Woof!' and the red shoes and 'I need some money.'

It was not hard for him to imagine Baby being just as happy with another man, for she seemed to see men as interchangeable. But Bunt could not picture himself with anyone except Mei-ping, for there was no one like her and, when he was with her, there was no one like him.

'First time in Macao?' the driver asked.

'Who wants to know?' Bunt said.

Mei-ping was sitting at an unrestful angle on the car seat still tipped against him.

'After Bela Vista you want to visit casino?'

Bunt said, 'We'll see,' and out of the window saw a brilliant floodlit fortress wall and several pedestals.

'They take the statues, they send them to Portugal so they don't get broken by the Chinese people,' the driver said. Then he spoke in Cantonese to Mei-ping, probably saying the same thing, but she did not reply.

The story that the statues and the treasures and the church relics had been famously bundled up and sent away was told all over Hong Kong as an example of the way in which the Portuguese colony was lying down and letting China have its wicked way with it – and that was a few years off. Hong Kong sneered at Macao, but Hong Kong had surrendered without a fight. Now, on the verge of leaving, Bunt wondered why the Hong Kong statues had not been sent back – Queen Victoria, Sir Thomas Jackson, Napier, and all the rest, including the Noon-Day Gun.

Up a steep street, a series of sharp turns, now on cobblestones, passing garden walls and painted mansions, with a view of the harbor and a narrow bridge. It was as though they had traveled from a Chinese port to a suburb of Lisbon.

The hotel was a large white villa at the edge of a cliff, and it was brightly lit, with gleaming floors and paintings in gilt frames; but it was empty. A woman in a dark jacket approached them.

'Checking in?'

'Two for dinner,' Bunt said, and stole a look at the embroidered badge on her jacket, hoping that it was one from Imperial Stitching. He could not tell.

'This way, please.'

Mei-ping followed flat-footed like a captive, looking fearful again. Perhaps it was the strange surroundings – there was no hotel like this in Hong Kong; perhaps the wooden floors looked unsafe to her.

Bunt ordered roast beef and vegetables and a bottle of claret from the large menu with dangling tassels. Mei-ping did not even glance at the menu.

'And madam?'

'Soup,' she said.

When the waiter had gone, Bunt said, 'That badge,' and tapped his chest. 'Is it ours?'

'Number seven. Special order. Four color, with gold highlight,' Mei-ping said in a funereal voice, reminded again of the factory and Ah Fu.

The wine was uncorked and poured. Bunt toasted: 'To us.' But Mei-ping still looked sad.

Bunt said, 'I will look after you.'

'How he got into my room?' Mei-ping said.

'Never mind,' Bunt said.

He drank and was happy. He knew that he had the means to protect her. Mei-ping sat, round-shouldered, with the soft face of a sad kitten, poking her spoon into her soup. Bunt could tell that this was not her idea of soup. That dense stew of dumplings and sodden greens and fish balls at the Golden Dragon, served up by Hung: that was her idea of soup, and she had paid for it. Bunt tore his meat apart and watched its watery blood run out when he cut it, and he chewed it and swallowed the beef-colored wine and wiped his lips.

'Please don't worry,' Bunt said.

They had their coffee on the verandah, sheltered from the wind by the shutters. Macao lay below and beyond – the harbor, the casinos, the clubs; small bright lights and the shadows of rooftops, the outlines of slopes. It seemed a place that had already been abandoned by the Portuguese colonialists and had not yet been occupied by the Chinese.

'I am sorry,' Mei-ping said at last.

It was what Bunt wanted to hear: she recognized that she was a problem, that she had a dilemma; and he was looking after her, he had the answer.

Still holding the last of a glass of wine he would not waste, he said, 'You can trust me. I will always look after you.'

His sincerity seemed to win her confidence – and why not? He had never said such a thing to any woman. The beauty of being with bar girls was that you never told them the truth, because they did not care what you said. Yet it surprised him to think that he was happy saying it to her, that he took pleasure in this. He desired her, but he could be patient. There was no hurry. What mattered most was that she felt safe with him, and it did seem that she was more relaxed right now.

Another swig of wine: in that mouthful he could taste the word love on his tongue. He swallowed it and sipped again and the word was in his mouth again. He wanted to tell her this good news. It was an appropriate moment, the lights playing on the creamy columns of the hotel verandah, all of Macao spread out in the distance, the palm fronds rattling just beneath them. The air was mild and delicately perfumed by some flowers he could not see.

Macao was poor and submissive and strange and spare; quieter than Hong Kong, with a sadness about it. That was welcome now. This hotel was where they belonged. Bunt had always believed that Hong Kong was his home, but no: he was a visitor and so was Mei-ping, and it was time to leave. And the truth was – he saw it tonight – if you loved someone you could live anywhere, because they were your life, no matter where you were.

Bunt said, 'I want to get a room here. Please don't worry.'

Mei-ping simply stared at him, her hands in her lap, her straight black hair framing her pale face. Once she had told him, 'When my hair is too short I look like man.' She was wrong. She cut it and she looked like a boy, and that made Bunt even more amorous.

Still staring, she was a thin boy on the edge of her chair. She had not moved her hands. Bunt took the position of her hands to mean yes.

They were checked in by the clerk at reception, who wore the blazer and the Imperial Stitching badge. She attempted to read his poor handwriting.

'Neville Mullard,' he said.

'And that's a double,' the woman said.

When had they stopped using the word wife?

'Our bags are being sent on,' Bunt said.

'I will tell Ollie to watch for them.'

Near a potted palm and an old framed map, Ollie stood to attention and saluted. He too had a blazer badge from Imperial.

The room faced the sea. Bunt opened the curtains wider and saw that Mei-ping was seated in an armchair looking out. He turned off the bedside light and was soothed by the way the room was illuminated by the colored lights of Macao. Bunt stood behind Mei-ping's chair with his hands resting on her shoulders. He meant to reassure her. After a few moments he made a suggestion using the pressure of his hand, and helped her up. He led her to the part of the bed that was in shadow.

Mei-ping lay clothed upon the coverlet, her small hands folded on her chest, staring at the veils of light that flickered on the high ceiling. Bunt did the same. Parallel, silent, stretched out, they were like the marble effigies of a knight and his lady on a tomb in a church he had seen once on a visit to England – not far from Uncle Ron's in Worthing. He had been so small he'd had to get inside the railings and stand on tiptoes to see them properly. He had always remembered that they were clothed, that they wore headgear – the man a helmet, the woman a bonnet. He had been impressed by the position of their feet, the toes turned upright. It remained for him a marble image not of death, but of marriage, sliding through life side by side, and until now he had never believed he would know such horizontal harmony and happiness.

The only noise tonight was the tooting of ships' horns, and then a motorbike bumping on the Portuguese paving stones, and his own breathing. No sound came from Mei-ping. There they lay, and the lights that shifted on the ceiling also lit the two of them. Mei-ping's thin dress clung to the flat planes of her body and showed her pretty bones. Bunt sensed again that she was warm: though their bodies were not touching the heat reached him.

'Are you all right?' he asked.

'Yes,' she said. It meant everything.

The trance took over, and he could still taste the wine with the word love in it, as though the wine was a rare form of ink from which beautiful words were written on his flesh. Blood was another sort of ink: different words. *Yes*, he thought, *I am drunk.*

'I am so happy.'

He seemed to be sitting outside the passage of time, unaffected by it, in a zone without clocks. He knew he was changed for good. His posture was a vow – flat on his back, hands held in prayer, face and toes upturned. Hers too. She missed her friend, but she would be happy when she allowed him to do as he wished. He saw himself with her again in the English house, a rainy day, looking out at the dripping trees. Mei-ping was not saying anything but she was happy. There were no other people in the house, there was no one in the garden, no one in the hills. Big logs were alight in the fireplace.

'Say something.'

'I was sad on the boat, because I saw something,' she said.

'What did you see?'

'Lantau Island. The village of Gou Chou Chew,' she said. 'I was there.'

'Living there?'

'Just stopping,' she said. 'My family is from Huizhou, on a river, something like fifty miles from Shenzhen. Cannot go into Shenzhen without a pass. Instead we go to Nantou, the port. West of Shenzhen.'

The names meant nothing to Bunt. He said, 'How old were you?'

'Ten years ago,' Mei-ping said.

Fifteen years old. He saw her clearly, skinny and small, in loose cotton clothes, wearing slippers, a kerchief tied on her head, a plastic satchel, the kind they all had.

'My auntie took me to a house in the village. She found a snake-head and paid him some money – almost a thousand – for a Fisherman's Permit. Then we waited. There are PLA guards in the daytime but not at night. We looked for a boat.'

A foghorn sounded in the harbor of Macao and it was so distinct it seemed as though it was coming from a ship that was tucked under the hotel.

'We found a fisherman who said he would take me. Anyone can travel on a fishing-boat with a permit, but only the snake-heads sell them. There were other women on board, many of them were pregnant – they wanted to come to Hong Kong for a better chance.'

Mei-ping's face was so smooth and so beautifully lighted it seemed to be carved from ivory. Even if she had not been speaking Bunt could have gone on looking at her, marveling at the fineness of her features.

'I was with the fisherman – he was steering the boat, and

it was very rough. Wind and waves. The mouth of the Pearl River is like the ocean. The boat was moving side to side and I could see nothing in the darkness. I was afraid we would be stopped. The captain said, "What is wrong with you?" and I told him I was afraid. He said, "I will tell them you're my daughter." He laughed and came near me and touched me.'

She stopped speaking a moment, she hesitated, as though trying to gain courage to continue. Soon she resumed.

'No one had ever touched me before that.'

Bunt said, 'Did you scream?'

Shaking her head, more in sadness than to indicate no, she said, 'I asked him, "Do you have a daughter?" He said nothing, so I knew the answer was yes. I asked him again, "Would you want a man to do this to her?"'

The purity of what she said moved Bunt: he could see it, the two figures contending in the wheelhouse of the fishing-boat.

'He was so ashamed,' Mei-ping said. 'In the early morning we came near some land. We jumped into the water – it wasn't deep. We were met by a snake-head. He took the rest of my money. I was so sad to have no money. Then I met Ah Fu. She had come on the same boat, but she was with the pregnant women. We helped each other. That was on Lantau Island, near Gou Chou Chew Village. I was so sad when I saw it today.'

That was as much as he could bear: he did not want to know more, not tonight. It upset him to hear her mention the fisherman making a pass, and the dignity in her reply.

Bunt raised himself up on one elbow and looked beyond Mei-ping to the window. Just past the shadow of the bluff below the hotel were the lights of the casinos. In this light he checked his watch. It was not yet eleven. An hour or more they had lain there, yet it was enough: now he knew he loved her.

'Let's have a flutter,' Bunt said.

She said yes, though she probably did not know the word. In the taxi he placed his hand on hers. He could feel the pressure of her fingers responding to his, and he was delighted.

Five or six tall blonde women in black leather jackets were standing near the taxi rank at the Lisboa Hotel, where Bunt and Mei-ping got out. The taxi driver took an interest. He smiled. He had some gold among his teeth. He said, 'Russians!' The women were fox-faced and pale. They simply stood, while the smaller Chinese people bustled around them. They had gray eyes and sword-like bones showing in their legs and high-heeled shoes. So single-minded were the Chinese passing among them, intent on entering the casino to gamble, that hardly anyone seemed to notice them.

'I feel sorry for them,' Mei-ping said in a whisper. 'They are not happy.'

Bunt did not want to know why. He steered Mei-ping inside the Lisboa and watched her face fall as she entered the inner gateway of the casino.

The gamblers were grubby punters, and few were Hong Kong people – probably not from Macao either. They were mostly hard-faced Chinese with dirty hands and spiky hair, in old clothes, from over the border – Zhuhai people, Cantonese stall-holders and hawkers, butchers, factory hands, hustlers, even farmers. Many of them looked as though they had just chucked a hoe or a pitchfork aside, let go of a wheelbarrow, walked out of a cabbage field. Even their clothes were dirty and torn. They smoked heavily.

They had thick doubled-over wads of money, held together by rubber bands, the sort of wide rubber bands they used to bind chickens' legs when they carried the birds to market.

They shouted, they spat, they dumped chips on the tables. They stacked their chips in tottering towers so that croupiers could easily rake them into a drawer. They made gambling seem no more than a sudden irrational discarding of money, people ridding themselves of filthy hundred-dollar notes, and grunting as they flung them aside.

Mei-ping looked on without any expression, but when Bunt glanced at her she smiled – at last. It was the longest period of time they had ever spent together, and though he had it in his mind to make love to her, he had hardly touched her. Yet in this vulgar Portogee clip-joint in Macao, in the dense cigarette smoke, among the Russian whores and frenzied gamblers, Bunt felt only sweetness towards Mei-ping, and sweetness towards the world. He saw that love had to be generous. He wanted to make love to Mei-ping, but not only that. He wished for her to be happy. He loved her for her nervousness, for the way she cared about her friend, for her distraction and her helplessness and her history, for the way she accepted his attention. She was a fifteen-year-old who had sailed from China alone in a fishing-boat, and had waded ashore at Lantau Island. She was better than he was – stronger, more decent, much nicer.

'Let's win some money.'

'Yes.'

'Then go back to the hotel.'

'Yes.'

'Yes' was the most beautiful word in the language and in his happy stupor of love it filled him with joy.

Blackjack was a game he understood. He bought five hundred dollars' worth of chips, then wandered among the tables watching games in progress, cards being dealt, chips stacked and swapped and raked, and at last taken away with a clicking sound that was so final. Bunt slid onto a stool and placed his bet, signaling to the dealer that he wanted to play.

He had chosen a table where five other women in black sat with their heads bowed like a coven of witches.

Mei-ping stood behind him. He could feel the pressure of her body against his back. Only since early that evening had he learned to love the closeness of her body and gain strength from it. He watched the clean playing-cards being slipped smoothly from the shuffler box by the dealer, who was a woman with the sort of fingers that were useful in a firm that did stitching and weaving. He knew the physical traits that marked a good worker – the deft fingers, the good posture, keen eyesight and concentration, the hand and eye coordination. Any of these dealers, he knew, would have been productive factory workers.

He folded three times. Then on his fourth hand he was dealt a six, a ten – he turned the cards slowly, peeking first, as the other players did, keeping their heads down. Should he fold again? He knew what he needed, but it was a long shot. Yet gambling was not gambling when it was safe, only when everything was risked, all for love. And so he put all his chips in a stack and tapped his fingers to indicate Hit Me. The card was slipped face down from the shuffler and pushed towards him. He turned it over: a five.

'Yes!'

An instant later, from the coven of black-clothed witches he heard, 'Bunt?'

It was his mother, sitting in the midst of the women, all the rest of whom were Chinese, yet she greatly resembled them. She had just lost the hand on his turn of the card, and her pillar of chips was being swiftly removed. Bunt had not seen her, nor she him. But she knew his voice, that strangled cry of triumph.

Collecting his winnings, three stacks of red chips, he said, 'Mother, this is Mei-ping.'

'Fancy that,' she said, and coughed into her fist. 'I'm about done, Bunt. Let's catch the next jet-foil back to Hong Kong.'

'We were going to stay a titch longer.' He thought of the room at the Bela Vista, the bed, the high ceiling, the view of the harbor.

'Don't be silly, Bunt. Take my bag – there's a good chap.' She had already turned to go. 'Stop faffing around and come along. You too, duckie.'

Mei-ping stared at her, and then followed.

THIRTEEN

The interior of the jet-foil, as it shook across the water to Hong Kong in the dark, was damp and foul-smelling, odors of damp smoky clothes and sea-fog, the treacly hum of engine oil; even the loud and vibrating hull stank of its crusted iron, a sour aroma of rust, like old fruitcake. From time to time a passenger would loudly clear his throat and spit. To the Chinese the visible world was a spittoon.

Bunt shut his eyes, refusing to look at where the thing landed. The jet-foil held in its stale air the passengers' bitter emotions too – their anger, their low temperature, their sour frowns of defeat, of having been cheated, which was a kind of sickness. Nearly all of them stank with a sense of grievance and loss. Gamblers on their way home, parched and hung-over, all of them losers.

The whole experience of cadaverous jammed-in people was akin in Bunt's mind to spending an hour in a mass grave. His mother, asleep, gave the appearance of being dead – and of having died violently – her head lolled and her legs splayed and her arms and hands twisted and positioned, as though she had just been murdered while fending off her attacker.

Bunt was miserable. The sight of Mei-ping staring at the bulkhead only made him more disconsolate. Was she reading the sign fixed to the bracket? It gave instructions for action in a possible accident, with life-jacket particulars lettered in two languages, *In Case of Emergency* – and then some business about 'Muster Stations.' In every corner the most innocent-seeming detail seemed to speak darkly of the Handover. Not only the emergency sign and the muster stations, what about the placard in front of his mother advertising *Speedy Chinese Take-away*?

'What's wrong?' Bunt asked, but hopelessly, because he knew.

Still staring, Mei-ping said, 'I have nowhere to go.'

Deeper than their sudden departure from Hong Kong, which was just cruel, her grief was Hong Kong dog, a fever of almost fathomless woe. It was the knowledge that the way forward was indistinct in part because the Hong Kong person had no visitable past. One of the imperatives of living in Hong Kong was that everyone tried to concoct an escape route, whether it was a foreign passport or a relative in Canada or a marriage of convenience. Mei-ping's despair was not so much that she found it hard to imagine her future, it was – more painfully – that she could not go back. She could not return to China. She had fled on the fishing-boat; somehow she had survived the captain and the snake-heads. China was a hole: no one ever went back, for fear of being buried alive. Hers was the worst of the Hong Kong dilemmas – she could not go forward or back. And her apartment was now dangerous.

Bunt understood her problem better than anyone, because he understood her. He had the solution, though it was still a bit premature to explain it to her. It meant fleeing for good. It would work, because fleeing was in Mei-ping's nature. He needed her fearlessness in this respect, to show him how to pick himself up and go. Without her he felt no desire; with her he was a tiger. She had the passion and the guts; he had the destination. If she didn't like England they could try another country. He could prove to her that you could go anywhere if there were two of you, for then you were never alone, and your mother was somewhere else.

'Go to Kowloon Tong,' he said, leaning over and whispering to Mei-ping. 'Stay at the factory. There's a cot in my office and some food and water in the fridge. The microwave's in Miss Liu's room. She has noodles. You'll be fine.'

Mei-ping was still staring at the diagrams and the warnings in the *In Case of Emergency* sign that was bolted to the bulkhead in front of her face. She had a small boy's solemnity: narrow shoulders, a slender neck, a small boy's head, even to the wisps of hair in her eyes.

'Here's a key,' Bunt said, detaching it from his key ring and passing it to her, as his mother, still looking mugged, sighed in her sleep.

The manner in which Mei-ping took the key, the pressure of her fingers and the trick of its vanishing in her hand was her way of saying yes. He liked her stuck-out schoolboy's jaw and her refusal to see him smiling fondly at her. He knew that she trusted him.

'On Monday we'll make another plan,' he said.

She had stopped mentioning the police. There were certain situations that arose in Hong Kong, usually Chinese situations, nearly all to do with the triads or the gangs or the secret societies, that were beyond the reach of the police. This was no gang, but Hung's secrecy and his confidence were menacing in that way. The whole of China was a secret society. For Mei-ping it was no longer a matter of finding Ah Fu now but of saving herself. This was not the time to discuss any of this – the Macao jet-foil at midnight? the stale fruitcake stink of the hull? the spitting? his mother looking battered? Besides, Mei-ping was afraid, and she was proud, and Bunt was being her benefactor. She needed face.

The jet-foil slowed and sank lower and bumped at the terminal. Betty woke, smacking her lips, making grotesque faces as she adjusted her teeth. Then she reached for her bag, and thrashed to get herself upright.

Every arrival in Hong Kong – train, tram, bus, van, ferry, tube – was treated by all passengers as though it was an evacuation on the verge of pure panic. This was no different: people mobbed the narrow exit door. Mei-ping made way for Betty, Bunt noticed with approval, though Betty didn't see it – she too was elbowing her way off the gangway, muttering, 'Chinese fire drill.'

'Bye for now,' Bunt said.

Mei-ping, looking squarely at him, raised her pretty hand in farewell. She held her other hand against her dress, and that hand was closed, holding the key. She gave nothing away, either in her expression or her posture. Bunt was proud of her for being able to possess such secrets. He marveled at her and his admiration of her became a general admiration for the crowd, for everyone had secrets in Hong Kong – true secrets that were akin to mysteries, for they were never revealed.

'Come along, Bunt.'

As the crowd of people hurrying towards Central surged around her, and she was lost among those people, Bunt strained to see her, to indicate to her that he cared. The Chinese 'Last Look' was so important to her. He could not find her face.

'Bunt!'

His mother began to grumble in advance at the thought of the taxi. Bunt resented her insistence on dragging him away from Macao, hated the idea that he had to come home with his mother. He was prevented from being with the woman he loved on the very night he planned to tell her he loved her.

Of all people, Mei-ping would understand. It was Chinese to look after your mother. It was Chinese for dull duty to separate you from pleasure. It was Chinese not to say the thing that was in your heart, Chinese to say 'I don't know' when you knew, Chinese to love in silence, Chinese to reveal nothing of your feelings, especially when they were passionate. And so his leaving her in this mood of Chinese contradiction, saying nothing whatever of what he felt, he knew she would read as his desire to stay with her, to love her, to marry her, to take her away. At the moment of their Chinese separation they had never been closer.

In his bed back at Albion Cottage he arranged his long body with his feet sticking up and he folded his hands on his chest and stared at the ceiling, as he had done so happily at the Bela Vista, in the manner of the marble figures on the English tombs.

He prayed that Mei-ping was doing the same thing in Kowloon Tong. It was Chinese to suffer, Chinese not to complain, Chinese to sink into the crowd. At his Last Look – not the last one he had attempted, but the last successful one, straining and raising himself up – she was moving through the crowd (he saw her head) like a lost boy. *I love you.*

In the morning he woke with the intention of hurrying to Imperial Stitching to see Mei-ping. He entered the lounge and saw his mother drinking tea at the breakfast table. She was reading the *Sporting News*, circling the names of likely horses, 'handicapping the ponies,' as she called it.

'Lucky us,' she said, looking down.

Racehorses had names like 'Lucky Us' and so it might have been one she liked the odds on; yet she was still talking in a drawling and self-satisfied way, as though to detain him. She did that sometimes, used her nagging as a net to snare him, threw up a wall of talk before him. And it had worsened lately into a sort of pompous garrulity. The deal with Mr

Hung had changed her outlook and made emphatic certain domineering traits of hers which had up to then been no more than lovable lapses of a funny old dear.

'I always thought your father was such a fool with his money. That bally factory.'

She smiled at Bunt and patted the chair next to her at the breakfast table.

'Mr Chuck,' she said. She was still ticking off horses' names, keeping her head down. 'Poor old Henners. Maybe it's true that you only miss people when they're brown bread, but if Mr Chuck hadn't turned up his toes would we be looking at a million quid and doing very nicely thank you? I think not.'

Again the word 'million' in her mouth made her seem such a buffoon; it was an even greater gaffe than all her clichés and rhyming slang. 'Million' was a good test of anyone who used it, 'million quid' even better. Bankers seldom said it, but passengers on the hard seats in the upper decks of trams clutching thirty-cent tram tickets mumbled 'million' all the time.

'We're laughing,' she said. 'Here, Bunt, have a cup of tea and your porridge before it gets cold. Wang!'

Wang entered, moving sideways in his round-shouldered way, smiling nervously and saying, 'Missy?'

'The master's wanting his porridge. And bring some more hot water for the pot, there's a good chap.'

When had he become 'the master'?

Bunt remained standing. He said, 'I was just going out.'

All he could think of was Mei-ping, her small head tilted slightly to hear his knock better, or the ring of the telephone.

To challenge him, his mother put out her jaw and swelled her jowls. She was a pale woman with a fleshy face that in repose was a pudding, but her expressions of disapproval seemed to mimic many of the recent British prime ministers whom Bunt knew from their photographs. His mother had cold Thatcher eyes and a Harold Wilson pout, a jaunty Jim Callaghan jaw and Edward Heath's pink beaky nose. She was Churchill now as she shook her jowls and put out her lower lip, and Bunt knew she meant no.

'But I've got to nip over to the factory.'

His mother kept her lip thrust out and said, 'You'll do no such thing, my poppet.'

'Mum,' he said, whining slightly.

'It's a race day,' she said.

'The road to Sha Tin will be chock-a-block!'

'Happy Valley,' she said. 'We'll take a taxi. Like old times.'

'The first race is at two-thirty,' he said, negotiating. 'I can easily be back from the factory by then.'

'Sit down and eat your breakfast, Bunt,' she said, lowering her head once more and studying the racing form. 'Monty's coming in an hour.'

'What's he want?'

With studied reluctance, as though he were forcing her to do it, she raised her face to him and gave him a smile of utter contempt.

'"What's he want?"' she said, mimicking him. (And Bunt thought: If Mei-ping and I ever have a child I will never ridicule him or mimic anything he says.) 'He wants to help us. He wants to discuss the sale of our factory. He wants to finalize the Hung business. Don't you see? He's liaising.'

'Liaising' was another word he never imagined his mother ever using, and he noticed with satisfaction that she sounded a total plonker as she said it.

'Hung's a creep,' Bunt said. 'Worse than a creep.'

'He is a buyer. We are the vendors. He has ready money. That is all that matters. And you call yourself a businessman?'

All this practical commercial wisdom from someone who had spent her life knitting jumpers and paying bookmakers, and showing her Chinese cook how to make oaties and how to knife the crusts from the edges of bloater paste sandwiches, and the way to butter the end of the bread loaf before sawing it off to produce a buttered slice.

'What do you know about Hung?'

'As much as I want to know. Now eat your breakfast.'

Over his porridge he fretted, rehearsing a possible trip to Kowloon Tong. If he did go this morning, what would he tell Mei-ping to calm her? There was nothing. She was safe there – she knew that, and as a long-time stitcher it was her second home in any case. He needed to act, to take her away. His fear had been that she would go to the police and accuse Mr Hung of killing Ah Fu. But he was fairly certain now that she wouldn't. She was too fearful to do that now, and she understood that while it was a tragedy that her friend was missing, she had him, Bunt, as compensation – more than that, a future.

Monty arrived at eleven, apologizing for his lateness, remarking on the view, saying what most people said when they saw the Peak Fire Station – 'You'll be in excellent shape if you have a fire, what with the fire brigade on your doorstep.' But seeing Monty unbuckling his briefcase in the lounge of Albion Cottage rather than in his office in Hutchison House made the sale of Imperial Stitching to Hung seem darker and more illicit and hugger-mugger. If his mother had become more pretentiously business-minded in an ill-informed way, and more inclined to gamble, Monty had come to seem devious and sinister. It was all Hung's corrupting influence.

Bunt sat by and watched his mother take charge, fussily, putting on her Maggie Thatcher face.

'When do we see our money?'

'It's a Third Party account,' Monty said. 'When all conditions are fulfilled, Full Moon will be compensated by the ministry, and then the disbursements will be made. You know the conditions.'

'Of course,' Betty said.

Bunt said, 'But I'm a dur-brain. Would you mind repeating the conditions?'

'I explained a while back that you are required to be out of the territory when the transfer is made. I will hand over the keys when the check is cleared. Full Moon will disburse the funds, minus closing costs, arrearages and stamp duty.'

Wang was pouring tea, making a business of it, Bunt felt, filling the pot with hot water, tapping the leaves out of the tea strainer.

'You said "territory."'

Monty stared at him as though he was the simpleton he claimed to be.

'You mean "colony."'

'What's the difference, squire?'

Bunt turned away from Wang, who was setting down a fresh pot of hot water, and said, 'It is a colony, in spite of what anyone in the British government says.'

Now both his mother and Monty were looking at him as though he was a lunatic.

'I go all queer when I hear the word territory,' Bunt said. 'It means surrender. Call it a territory and it's easier to hand over.'

'Spare us the Chinese Take-away,' his mother said.

'I thought you'd back me up,' Bunt said.

'He's narked because I wouldn't let him go across to the factory this morning,' his mother said to Monty: Mother moaning about her child in a snit. 'We're going to the races.'

He would seem even more childish if he argued, and so Bunt said, 'What guarantees are we getting that the work-force will be looked after?'

'One would imagine the usual guarantees implicit in the sale of a company to a Chinese entity,' Monty said.

'Does that mean none?'

'Did I say none?'

Bunt said, 'Any idea when this deal is going to happen?'

'We're looking at Monday for the issuing of the check.'

'So soon,' Bunt said, and thought of Mei-ping.

'About time,' his mother said.

'Thank you, Missy,' Wang said, and walked backwards into the kitchen.

Wang had begun to call his mother 'missy' at about the same time she had taken to calling Bunt 'the master.'

'Your house-boy is first-class,' Monty said, and yanked and fastened the buckle on his briefcase.

'He's a treasure,' Betty said.

'That's it, then. I will authorize your tickets out of Full Moon funds,' Monty said. 'As you might imagine, you are quite creditworthy.'

Bunt said, 'What I don't understand is why do you trust this creepy guy Hung?'

'I don't trust him,' Monty said. 'There's no deal until the check is cleared and you're paid.'

Bunt said, 'So it's just a matter of money. If he's got the money and we're paid he's to be trusted. Ha!'

But no one else was laughing, and Monty was staring at Bunt as he had a bit earlier, in a pitying way.

'Of course,' the solicitor said. He was not smiling. His eyes were dead. He was bored and wanted to go. 'This is strictly business, squire.'

'Now Bunt and I are going to the races,' Betty said. 'Aren't we, Bunt?'

Bunt was a little boy. He was unreliable and a bit stupid. He liked treats, the way little boys did. Mother and son, off to the races.

*

Just like a child, just like old times – yet he tried not to think of all the confidences he had exchanged with his mother in the Members' Enclosure at Happy Valley. Wang had packed a hamper – cold chicken salad, smoked salmon and paste sandwiches, slices of cake, some fruit, three bottles of stout, napkins: a picnic.

Seeing the hamper and being told the destination, the taxi driver said, 'A nice day for you – food and sunshine. And you lucky, I think.'

The driver was cheery in an envious and salivating way, glancing at them in the rear-view mirror. Over the years so many times strangers like this, drivers usually, summed up the situation and delivered such a judgment, saying how lucky they were, Bunt and his mother. And they were never right – ever, ever. What they saw and what pleased them was the opposite of the truth. Their compliments were like mockery.

But just as he was at his most resentful, the taxi came to a stop in race-day traffic on an overpass into Happy Valley. His mother gave him a pat on the cheek.

'Poor Bunt. I know you don't want to be here.'

'No, I do, Mum,' he protested, his voice shrill with his lie.

Betty laughed softly. She said, '"Nip over to the factory" – is that the expression young people use these days?'

Her knowing expression made Bunt turn away. She had made him feel sheepish, but why? He loved Mei-ping. He did not want her to be his Chinese secret.

'What's her name?' Betty said, and giggled a little.

'It's not like that,' Bunt said, but he was pleased by the mild way his mother had asked, not out of wickedness but in a spirit of sympathy.

'You can drop us here,' Betty said to the driver, who had been eyeing them in the mirror. 'Take the hamper, Bunt.'

His mother walked ahead, holding her member's pass and jumping the long queue of Chinese who were waiting at the turnstile. In spite of himself, Bunt was a bit happier. His mother had just been nice to him.

The Members' Enclosure was filling with people and several women acknowledged Betty in a familiar way. They were wearing old-fashioned hats – flowers on the brim of one, ribbons and a great green bow on the other. They batted Chinese fans at their chins. Bunt was impressed by their sisterly tone. He had the posh-common accent of the colony, jumped up like his mother. He had hardly ever taken notice of such people. His life had been the factory, his mother, the bar girls, and he had disliked the expression 'British community' for the way it seemed to lump him with all the plonkers – clerks and soldiers, and twits and tarts, as though they existed in a tight little group of people, refugees from the UK, wagging the flag and grubbing for business, and agreeing on just about everything. Yet it was not the case in Hong Kong and probably had never been.

Yet whatever it had been, it was ending. Royal Hong Kong, the Crown Colony, the Union Jacks stretched out in the wind over the police stations, the portraits of the Queen in post offices, the policemen themselves in their panda cars and bobbies' helmets, the reassuring red vans lettered in gilt *Royal Mail*. And this place, the Happy Valley Race Course, the Royal Hong Kong Jockey Club, all these people gathered under the British flag in the Members' Enclosure – it was almost over.

Perhaps it was the right thing to do, what he was doing. If the deal was closing and the check cleared and they were out of Hong Kong on Monday, then he had to be here in Happy Valley among the smug and seedy-faced Brits, for this was in a profound way a ritual of farewell. He would never have another chance. It was appropriate that he was here with his mother, and he was touched when he recognized it as a ritual, for all rituals were symbolic approximations of real acts – and all the sadder for being approximate. But more than anything this ritual was important as an ending. Under any other flag it would have been a travesty. He needed to be here as a witness, for wasn't this the last British colony?

'I'm peckish,' Betty said. 'I wonder whether Wang remembered the sandwiches.'

She was rooting in the hamper.

'Sarney?'

'I won't say no.'

'Smoked salmon?'

'Paste,' Bunt said.

The chairs creaked, the awning flapped and so did the women's hat brims and their paper fans, the flags flew, and in the distance they could hear the loudspeaker: *No wagers will be accepted after* . . . The crowds howled in the stands, while the vast movie-screen-sized T V monitors showed the horses being walked through the gauntlet of owners and officials. It would all end, in spite of the Chinese promises. It was nearly over even now. Nothing in Britain's history had ever ended like this – Hong Kong and its people were part of the Chinese Take-away. Bunt had not fully comprehended this until now; Happy Valley helped him understand the Imperial Stitching sale, which he now realized was not a sale at all, but a hand-over to Hung, and he was moved.

'I'm glad I came,' Bunt said.

'Eh?'

When his mother's mouth was full and she was working her teeth over the food, she often complained that the chewing deafened her. There were flecks of smoked salmon on her lips, her cheeks bulged. She could not hear a thing.

Bunt waited and after she swallowed he repeated what he had said.

'Good boy,' his mother said. Her newspaper was folded efficiently to display the racing columns she had annotated. 'Now finish your sarney and then place some bets for your poor old Mum, won't you?'

He ate. He went to the window and placed his mother's bets as he had been instructed. A Quinella in the first race, and a Double Quinella in the next two, hedged by a Six Up, which covered six races. And then he collected the betting slips and returned to his chair and looked at the horses and the race officials, the exaggerated frenzy of the Chinese gamblers, the self-conscious serenity of the English women, his mother's friends in the Members' Enclosure.

The horses shot out of the gates, and the violence of it, the sight of the screen, the howls of the crowd, made him remember Mei-ping's nightmare of execution – Ah Fu being led out by the soldiers of the Chinese army to be shot in the back of her neck. He could see the very spot where she would be kneeling, and from the position of the horses the way she would be shown on the screen. He saw only Ah Fu collapsing onto her side, blood streaming from her neck, not the galloping horses.

'You're not watching the race,' his mother said.

'Yes, I am.'

'Who won?'

'I don't know.'

'See.'

But she was not scoring a point. Her smile was maternal, forgiving, concerned.

'What's wrong, Bunty?'

Something within him clutched at his vitals, knotting them like a cramp. That was a tight twist of pain. He felt weak and worried. He had a secret – more than one, and he was no longer strong enough to keep them.

He said, 'I don't know what to do.'

It was all he needed to say. The rest was up to his mother. When he said it, Betty seemed to relax. She looked him up and down. It was as though he was a strange edifice that she had happened upon, like any of the new confusing buildings in Admiralty and Central, and she was looking for an approach – a footpath, a stairway, a bridge, a ramp, revolving doors, an arch; a way of gaining entry.

'It's your Chinky-Chonk, isn't it?'

He said nothing and his silence was yes.

'From Macao?'

Nothing again, like a nod.

'Chinese, mum. Her name is Mei-ping.'

'I had an inkling,' she said, and offered him another sandwich. He shook his head no. She put the package of sandwiches down and leaned nearer. 'She seems such a sweet little thing. One of the cutters, isn't she?'

'Stitchers.'

'I fancy,' Betty said – a little uncertainly because she was chewing – 'I fancy she was at that dinner with Hung.'

He could not reply. The mention of the Golden Dragon dinner filled his head with images. Chicken feet. Entrails. Mr Hung's teeth. A trussed and screaming woman.

'That's when it started.'

Another race had begun. Horses with tangled manes and jockeys clinging to their necks flashed onto the screen, and their hoof beats were transmitted through the turf. Bunt could feel this sound pulsing against the soles of his feet.

Betty sat back and said, 'When that girl went missing.'

Bunt sucked a breath through his nose, another way he had of indicating yes.

'Ah Fu,' he said, to give her a name.

'And I said, "I shouldn't be bothered."'

He nodded.

'But after a bit you asked Mr Hung about the missing girl.'

'In a way,' he said in a croaky voice.

'And you got no joy,' his mother said.

He had pressed his lips together so as to prevent himself from speaking again. But it was futile because this way his thin lips indicated that he was in a muddle.

'And now your friend, this girl Mei-ping, wants to go to the police,' his mother said.

She showed genius in her intuition, her sense of smell alone was almost unnatural, like that of an animal downwind which raises its head at a vagrant aroma leaking from far away. Bunt knew that he was not able to conceal anything from her, and with instincts like that his mother might be able to help.

'It's worse than that,' Bunt said. 'All of Ah Fu's belongings have disappeared. Mei-ping is petrified. That's why I took her to Macao – to calm her.'

He looked at his mother. Yes, she believed him.

'She is afraid of Hung,' he went on. 'Hung wants to find her.'

'The man is busy. Why would he want that?'

'Because she is the only person who saw him with Ah Fu. I mean, apart from me. She saw him leave the restaurant. If she went to the police she could describe how Ah Fu went missing – and then all her clothes, everything.'

Betty had lifted her binoculars and was holding them in the direction of the track, though no race was in progress just then. She said in a voice of unconcern, 'But she's not going to go to the police.'

'She might,' Bunt said. 'I wouldn't blame her. All the signs point to Hung.'

A new race started. Betty kept her binoculars trained on the track.

'I wish I had the guts to report him,' Bunt said.

'It would be the end of our deal,' Betty said, still following the horses.

'There'll be other deals.'

'There is only one Mr Hung.'

'He's a beast,' Bunt said.

'Oh, your Mei-ping will be fine,' Betty said in a shushing voice. 'She's back in her own little flat.'

'No,' Bunt said. 'Mum, this is serious.'

He was antagonized by the way she was watching the race as she carried on this conversation – not looking at him, fiddling with the knob on her binoculars. It distracted him, it made him talk loudly, especially now as the race was ending.

'She's staying at the factory,' Bunt said. 'I'm worried about her. Mum, are you listening?'

To the cheering and the sight of a single horse triumphant on the screen, Betty took her binoculars from her eyes and smiled at him.

'I think you're in love,' she said.

'Why are you smiling?'

She showed him the betting slip. '"Full Moon." I won.'

What a very strange woman she was, to be sure. Just a few days before collecting her substantial share in the one-million-pound deal for Imperial Stitching in Kowloon Tong, she won twenty-six Hong Kong dollars on a horse in Happy Valley, and she was speechless with jubilation. But his mother was a superstitious pagan with Chinese instincts, and this was a ritual: it was the name of the horse that mattered. Full Moon's victory was auspicious; it foretold that the deal would be a success.

That was her wager. Bunt's was a gamble too, for now

he had told her everything, and she was smiling. He felt better. He too had won.

The rest of the afternoon they spent in this way in the Members' Enclosure. Betty greeted more of her friends – they saw the hamper and Betty praised Wang again. They ate the chicken. They drank the stout, they ate the cake, they emptied the hamper. *The horses will go on running*, the Chinese dictator had famously promised. But no – they would be different horses, and Mei-ping was right: Happy Valley was more appropriate to executions. It was not just the end of this race day. This was the end of Hong Kong.

It was growing dark when they got back to the cottage. The taxi driver said, 'Nice view.' They all said that.

'I could murder a cup of tea,' Betty said. And she called out, 'Wang!'

There was no reply. She called out again, this time angrily, her features distorted, chewing her teeth as she waited for his answer. Nothing. She went to his room as though for the relief it afforded her to vent her anger – slam doors and stamp on the floor and kick the furniture and squawk. Then she was back, puzzled, still chewing.

'He's hopped it.'

FOURTEEN

Betty was muttering 'Bumhole' as Bunt went through the house to see whether Wang had stolen anything from them – the canteen of silver, George's gold watch, the musical-box, the jewel case, the monogrammed sugar tongs, George's RAF insignia, Betty's winnings from last week's race, the crystal table lamp, the horse brasses. Wang had not, and so the valuables seemed less valuable for being ignored and left untouched by the Chinese cook. The watch she remembered as gleaming was tarnished, so were the horse brasses, one tong was twisted. Again she muttered, 'Bumhole.'

Wang's small room at the back was empty, all his clothes were gone, only the evidence of his melancholy frugality remained – scraps of saved coupons, bus tickets, paperclips, a clutch of wire hangers in his closet, an old jam jar he used as a teacup, a broken comb, the cracked plastic sandals that set Bunt's teeth on edge when Wang scuffed through the house. He had always blamed Wang for his own horror of odd rice grains – Wang had retched at them and passed on to Bunt the anxiety that they might be maggots.

'Gone,' Bunt called out to his mother.

'Rat,' she said.

Another time, long ago, when they lived on Bowen Road, Bunt heard a man's screams from a nearby apartment house. Wang had said, 'He has cut off his own penis. Because he was very angry with his wife.' The man had screamed all night. Bunt was fifteen and Wang was also fifteen, in his first year as their house-boy. Betty had always seen their employing him as a sort of long-term rescue – a sacrifice on their part, a favor to him and his mother Jia-Jia that had gone on all these years.

So his disappearance showed the worst ingratitude, and he was conspicuously present in the empty space he had left behind: in that empty space were his stories, his superstitions, his talk, his fears, the odor of his cooking. And then standing there, troubled by all the ambiguous memories, Bunt's muddle was overtaken by a simpler and helpful impression that Wang's empty room resembled Ah Fu's. The room had been plundered of all her possessions – it had looked like this. The same rattly hangers, the same sweet-wrappers and cracked saucer, the same loose flakes of tea that had the look of squashed insects, the same circles from wet cups printed in interlocking O's on the tops of the side table and dresser, the same smell of soap and hair, the same yellowing mattress. And it was the same sort of disappearance, as sudden as an abduction. Irrationally, Bunt associated all disappearances with Hung – three of them, including Frank Woo the janitor, four if you included Mr Chuck. All these Chinese people had evaporated and left only residue.

He winced, thinking of Mei-ping, but his mother was talking.

'Wang never left even when I put the wind up him,' she said, 'so why would he hop it now?'

'Unless he somehow twigged we were going.'

'Not a chance.'

'He might have heard something,' Bunt said.

'Bumhole.'

'I was going to give him a going-away present,' Bunt said.

'A knuckle sandwich,' Betty said.

Nuckoo samwidge: Bunt laughed at her Balham expression and her Balham voice. He gave her a hug. Wang's departure was unexpected but it meant that they were now alone. By bolting, Wang had spared them feeling guilty and responsible for abandoning him. He had taken the initiative and abandoned them. They had dreaded telling him the news of their return to England. Would Wang scream? Would he cry, would he sulk? They did not know. The famously undemonstrative Chinese occasionally threw fits worthy of Italians. Betty had said, 'He might have gone spare.' But now the problem was solved.

Now they had the satisfaction of being free to despise him for leaving them, instead of feeling awkward about leaving him. Bunt especially had feared the onset of sentimentality – not just tears but money too, a bonus, severance pay, resettlement allowance. But Wang had jogged off on his own long legs, his skinny face set in his habitual snake-eyed stare.

'They're all alike,' Betty said.

Bunt was still staring at the emptiness, seeing Ah Fu's empty room.

'He's worried about the Chinese, his own people,' Betty said. 'It makes you think.' Then she nodded and her eyes hardened like Thatcher's as she added, 'Good riddance. We'll manage.'

It began to rain, just a scratching on the roof at first like a mass of hurrying rodents, as Betty made a pot of tea. She sat with Bunt in the lounge drinking it, defying Wang, and the rain came quicker: sky, ceiling, and roof were one. Betty was reminded of the storm the morning she got the news of Mr Chuck's death, remembered looking at the portrait of the Queen, remembered thinking that something important was ending. It had never entered her mind that it would be so dramatic as their own departure from Hong Kong. Events had moved apace. Mr Chuck's death was only the beginning

– there was so much more that had followed, that she could never have foreseen and had hardly influenced. That was how history happened: someone sneezed and died and everything followed, and you were part of it, and then you ended up watching and then you went home.

'Nice cup of tea,' Betty said. It was better than Wang's. Why had she put up with his muck all those years? *He's a treasure*, she had said to Monty, and others who had praised him, but she had never believed it. And now he was just a sneak and a hypocrite, and she suspected that he might also be insane.

Warming his hands on his teacup, Bunt had never felt closer to his mother. Betty switched on the Roberts: music from British Forces Broadcasting, Betty's favorite program, *West End Showcase*.

Hearing 'Some Day I'll Find You,' she said, 'I've always loved that song. George used to sing it.'

It was as though, saying that, she had forgiven him.

'Good day at the races,' Bunt said.

'I'm up a bit,' she said. 'But the most important thing was – we were together. Have an oatie, Bunt.'

'Won't say no.' He chose a crumbling oatie square from the plate and bit into it.

How odd Wang's oaties tasted now that the man was gone. He had baked them yesterday. They had a faint sour taste of Wang himself. Bunt could not finish his oatie. He put it down and was faintly disgusted by the sight of his teeth marks in it.

His mother had changed – so much had changed. She was no longer the bitter suspicious woman of the past. At first the combination of Mr Chuck's legacy and Mr Hung's proposition had confused her, and she had acted peculiar; but she was calmer now, mellower, much happier, her old motherly self, even ladylike, indulging herself in picnics and gambling. Bunt had been so thankful that she had listened sympathetically to his fears about Mei-ping. He trusted his mother now, and the simple English woman on this Chinese island was now to him as comfortable as an old sofa.

He said, 'I'm going to call Mei-ping. Just make sure she's all right.'

'Oh, yes. But I don't want you going out. It's a foul night.'

She was old-fashioned in the way she was always guided by the weather in the things she did. Fog and rain kept her indoors. 'My chest,' she said. Bunt hardly noticed the weather. She always commented when he returned home wet.

'What shall I tell her?'

'Anything you like.'

'About our leaving, I mean.'

'It's fixed for Monday.'

'You don't mind if she stops here tomorrow night?'

Betty thought a moment, seeming to make calculations with her teeth, moving them from side to side, like a primitive device for adding sums.

'She can have Wang's room.'

His mother was old-fashioned in that respect too. Bunt was forty-three years old. Mei-ping was the woman he planned to bring back to the UK, to marry – what else? Now he had to pretend they were not lovers. But that was a detail. All that mattered now was Mei-ping's safety. When they were in London what had seemed so urgent in Hong Kong would be forgotten. The question of Wendell being his half-brother was one that would only be asked as long as he was in Hong Kong. It could not be asked over the great distance to Britain. And as for Mr Chuck's legacy – the factory, Ah Fu, the missing Frank Woo, Mr Hung, the rest of it – all the Chinese problems would be China's problems.

Choosing carefully, because it was a refinement of his old

schoolboy fantasy, and now it included Mei-ping, he told his mother how he saw them living in a country house set in green meadows in the south of England.

'Surrey's lovely this time of year.' They had gone there on the train from Balham, she said. 'Change at East Croydon. We always got off at a station called West Humble and walked up Box Hill. The chalk slides. The blackberry bushes. All that grass. You could see for miles. The best bit was the gravestone.'

When she laughed on the word 'gravestone,' Bunt put his face in front of hers and said, 'Mum?'

'It was at the top of the hill, in that forest. The grave of a local chap. He was mental, I fancy. His dying wish was to be buried upside down, so that his head was facing China. Mine's the opposite!'

'Mum!' Bunt said, and then they were both laughing.

They would watch the Hong Kong Hand-over in that house in Leatherhead or Dorking. 'Good riddance,' she would say. 'Chinese Take-away.'

He called his office. Mei-ping did not answer. The answering machine clicked on. He hated his voice uttering the contradiction, *This is the Executive Office of Imperial Stitching. There's no one here at the moment, but your call is very important to us –*

After the beep he said, 'It's me – it's me – pick up the phone, May. I hope you can hear me. Please pick –'

'Yes,' Mei-ping said in a small voice.

'Are you all right?'

'I am afraid. Mr Hung want to find me.'

'He can't find you.'

'Someone might tell him.'

'No one knows – only me,' he said. 'Listen, May, I couldn't get over there today – I had to stay with my mother. I'll come tomorrow.'

'Yes,' Mei-ping said.

'We're leaving Monday for London. Please don't worry.'

This provoked a silence, which alarmed Bunt.

'Are you there?'

'Yes.'

'May, I told my mother everything. She knows about us. She's right here.'

Phoning another woman, one he loved, in his mother's presence gave him a confidence he had never felt before. He was at last a man.

'She's chuffed,' he said and looked across the room at his mother. In the poor light of the lounge he could not see his mother's face, but he knew she had to be smiling. 'She's over the moon. And May?'

'Yes.'

'No point in calling the police now.'

There was another silence, more worrying than the first one. Bunt spoke her name again.

'I am here,' she said. 'I am waiting for you.'

They were the most passionate words he had ever heard, and he thought: my life has just begun. He wanted then to say *I love you*, but something made him hesitate. Then his mother coughed – her full fruity cough: her chest, wet weather – and the spell was broken.

The next morning, Sunday, Betty was standing at the window saying, 'It's trying to rain – it can't make up its mind,' smiling at the fickle clouds hovering over China – the silly things. Bunt was indifferent, the weather did not matter any more, they were leaving it behind, another unreliable feature of Hong Kong, like Wang who had seemed so loyal just before he'd done a bunk.

'I'll bring Mei-ping back here before dinner,' Bunt said.

He had given up on Hong Kong, abandoned the factory,

he was in an England mood. He had his assurances, such as they were, from Monty. He did not want to think about the employees any longer.

'Change of plans,' Betty said, turning away from the window. She faced Bunt as she faced the clouds, with the same smiling expression, clicking her dentures.

'What do you mean?' he asked, and he would have been fearful had his mother not kept her smile. But her false teeth made her smile seem less sincere, even false.

'Hung's giving us lunch,' Betty said. She stooped and busied herself, sorting the Sunday *South China Morning Post* and its several sections. 'He rang first thing – while you were having your lie-in.'

Bunt was gabbling, trying to speak.

'I knew you wouldn't want to be woken up,' his mother said.

As always a sudden change of plans left Bunt in anguish, not merely confused but in pain. He felt naked and unprepared and did not know why. Canceled orders left him disturbed and forgetful, slightly blinded, and so he often lost his balance and stumbled a bit when he got bad news. Miss Liu at the factory might say *No, sorry, it's over here*, and shifting himself abruptly Bunt would usually hit his head. He needed to be prepared, he liked order, he loved the fantasies brought on by anticipation. An unexpected meal, even a great one, never tasted as good as one he had savored in advance. He thought his mother was just like him in this – and she had been, before. There was something slovenly about changing plans. You hesitated and looked a complete plonker.

'Tell her you'll pick her up afterwards,' Betty said. She spoke smoothly and it calmed him a little.

Again he needed to announce himself on the answering machine before Mei-ping picked up the phone.

'You sound tired,' Bunt said.

'I did not sleep. I was afraid.'

With his mother listening – at any rate, she was in the same room with him – he could not say what he was thinking: that he loved her, that he wanted to hold her, that their lives were beginning.

'I am coming to pick you up tonight. Everything is going to be fine.'

'I am waiting.'

FIFTEEN

The Golden Dragon again, Betty mumbling *Didn't we tell him we hate this food?* while large Chinese families were yakking at big round tables, another glimpse of old China. What was it about Hong Kong that allowed all these old habits to continue and flourish, as though it were a hot-house of heirlooms. Here they went on practicing their ancient rituals such as ancestor worship, feasting with their children and grandchildren, and squalling babies; giving each other cheesy presents and envelopes of money, in incoherent restaurants such as this.

Boisterous friendship and big families and gluttonous bingeing had continued in Hong Kong long after they had been banned in China as a social evil. In the Cultural Revolution they had disemboweled people for smiling or wearing pretty dresses or listening to the wrong radio station. Mr Chuck had told him all about it. The refugees, the aliens, the eye-eyes – all of them agreed that China was a nightmare, and now China was about to swallow them up. Maybe it was just what the Hong Kong Chinese deserved for having sneered at the British, who had not meant them any harm. *They don't work for me*, George Mullard had been fond of saying. *I work for them –*

There were no big families in China now. Children were illegal: you got shot or fined for having one nipper over the quota. But here the families were big and talkative – British

Hong Kong allowed it – the busy colony kept them all busy, and they were never livelier than among plates of sticky gleaming food, as they sparred and reached with their chopsticks.

Passing boisterous tables of Chinese holding bluepatterned bowls to their mouths, Bunt saw behind them a demon goddess with a crimson face in a shrine, lit by Christmas bulbs, with the offering on a plate in front of it, the usual orange: pure paganism. Noticing such things, and finding they grated on him, he realized it was time to leave.

Ahead, at a corner table as though in a remote part of China, Hung sat with Monty Brittain. Monty waved them over – he was active; Hung did not move. And just as Betty and Bunt took their seats, some food was brought and presented by a waiter pushing a trolley.

'Nothing personal,' Betty said, 'but we don't touch Chinese food. Never did. All the grease, all the glue. And it's always so wet. Makes me want to spew.'

'You see, it doesn't agree with us,' Bunt said.

Anyway, not eating would make this whole business move more quickly.

Monty said, 'Mr Hung would like to tell you something.'

Since when had Monty been in charge? London was still in his manner of speaking, though the man had an Austrian passport now and probably something to answer for. Bunt still felt insulted by the way Monty had persisted in asking him to renounce his citizenship and get a fuzzy-wuzzy passport.

Hung was looking froggy and solemn now that the deal was on the verge of closing. He simply sat there.

'Please eat something,' Hung said, as though he had not heard Betty describe her revulsion for Chinese food.

'They don't fancy it,' Monty explained.

At Hung's elbow, Monty seemed more Hung's solicitor

than their own. Bunt remembered how Monty had first introduced Hung at the Cricket Club, and later: *I proposed him. You've got to move with the times.* Monty it was who had warned him of Hung's gangster connection, the Chinese army hoodlums, the horrifying story of the dismembered solicitor. Monty knew so much – he was the sort of man who would stay, who had no allegiances underneath his banter, or if he had, they were certainly not British.

'I am happy with this business,' Hung said.

Betty and Bunt were sitting, not eating. *Even their tea isn't tea*, Betty used to say.

'But it is not good business if only I am happy. You must be happy also.'

'We're happy,' Betty said, and for the first time in the deal, clicking her teeth, did not look happy at all.

Perhaps sensing Betty's impatience, Hung winced, and then he looked at her with flinty eyes and fixing his lips in a sneer said, 'I have been kind and generous.'

Bunt said, 'Hang about. It was all a fluke. If Mr Chuck hadn't of died this never would have happened.'

Hung liked this. His laughter was a hairy rasping in his nostrils. He said, 'Please take a drink.'

'Orange squash,' Betty said. 'No ice.'

Hung waited until the orange squash was served to Betty, the glass presented on a white saucer. Betty glanced at it but did not drink.

'Mr Chuck took his last meal here,' Hung said, speaking with deliberate precision, as though each word mattered.

Bunt looked at Monty to whom this information did not seem to be news. In any case, Monty had not stopped eating.

'He was sitting where you are now,' Hung said, nodding at Betty. 'He seemed to enjoy his food.'

She said, 'Rubbish. He was nowhere near here. He died in his flat in Magazine Gap Road.'

'He was found dead in his flat,' Hung said.

'This is true,' Monty said, chewing, not looking up.

Bunt was cross with Monty for not challenging Hung. He faced Hung and said sharply, 'Here, did you have something to do with Mr Chuck?'

'I am merely saying we served him his last meal,' Hung said.

'Does "we" mean you are involved in this restaurant?'

Hung took his time in his reply. He had begun to sample bits of the meal, using his chopsticks like tongs.

'This restaurant belongs to the Chinese army. Many enterprises belong to the army. We own much of Shenzhen. Soon your factory site will be in our hands.'

At the mention of 'Chinese army' Betty seemed to come awake. She said, 'What's this all about then?'

Monty said, 'You are dealing with a man of considerable influence. Which is why I had no hesitation proposing him for the Cricket Club.'

'I am talking about Mr Chuck,' Betty said. 'He was my late husband's partner for years. Never put a foot wrong.'

'He was short-sighted,' Hung said, and raised his chopsticks to signal to Betty that he had not finished speaking. 'Your Mr Chuck would never have sold his share in Imperial Stitching to a China company.'

Bunt was listening with his hands clasped on his lap, leaning forward, wondering vaguely why they were still talking about Mr Chuck; but mostly he had Mei-ping on his mind.

'I told you,' he said. 'It was just a fluke.'

'But of course you were in his will,' Hung said.

'So we found out,' Bunt said, and stared, waiting for a reaction from Mr Hung. Seeing there was none, he went on, 'Did you know we were named in Mr Chuck's will? Because if you did –'

'This is getting us nowhere,' Monty said. He was chewing very rapidly, the way hungry animals ate when they knew there were other hungrier animals near them.

Betty said, 'I'm confused, Bunt. What are you saying?'

'Maybe Mr Chuck's death wasn't an accident.' His eyes were dancing in anger at Mr Hung, who seemed amused.

'Old history,' Mr Hung said.

'Please,' Monty was saying, using his chopsticks like a baton. 'Mr Hung has something to tell you.'

'You mean that's not it?' Bunt said.

Hung turned to Monty and said, 'Perhaps they will understand better if you explain.'

'You're leaving today,' Monty said. 'The money's being wired.'

Change of plans, his mother had said that morning, and it had thrown him, confused him and left him breathless. And that was only a meal that she meant – a dinner moved forward to lunch. This was something else, the departure from Hong Kong, and it was the same message, a change of plans. It gave Bunt chest pains and a sensation of vertigo. He wondered a moment whether he might be dying and if so it was murder.

He said, 'No, no.'

'But it's Sunday,' Betty said, being practical.

'It's Saturday in Grand Cayman,' Monty said. 'That's where Full Moon is registered. They're still transacting business. We've already had news of the transfer.'

'The rice is cooked,' Mr Hung said.

Betty's jaw stuck out at Mr Hung. It was a challenge made more dramatic by her having adjusted her bite. Slipping her dentures slightly gave her a look of wolfish defiance.

'It's a dog's dinner,' she said. 'There are no arrangements – no bookings, no tickets.'

'You're on the one-twenty Cathay Pacific flight to London. Confirmed seats. I've put you in First.'

'We've no tickets,' Bunt said.

'Here we are,' Monty said, digging into his briefcase. He produced a plastic wallet thick with itineraries and tickets, which he handed over. He said, 'Next question.'

In a trapped and fretful voice – he was breathing hard – Bunt said, 'We're not going anywhere. The deal's off. Mum?'

She was staring at Hung. She said, 'I don't think they're giving us much of a choice.'

'There is a choice,' Hung said. He was truculent, his English blunter and less elegant, even less fluent as he had become sulkier. 'You can leave now or you can wait and follow Mr Chuck. As for your factory – we own it now. In a sense we have always owned it.'

Bunt said, 'We'd like some assurances about the welfare of the employees.'

Hung was enigmatic when he sulked, but had an alarming smile. It was this smile that he turned towards Bunt, and then he calmly selected a toothpick and not changing his expression began working it between his teeth.

'Mum,' Bunt said again. He looked pitiable. He was reaching for his cellular phone. 'We can't.' And once more, 'Mum?'

Betty's expression, fixed on Hung, was one of fear and resignation, and yet she seemed in silence to be holding a conversation with him.

'I have to make a phone call,' Bunt said.

He dragged himself from the table and in the hubbub of the crowded restaurant, almost overwhelmed by the rising tide of chattering voices – the Chinese army owned this place? – he dialed his office at Imperial Stitching.

It rang and rang, and then the answering machine clicked on. *This is the executive office of Imperial Stitching . . .*

'It's me,' he said urgently. 'Please pick up the phone . . . May, please pick it up . . . Pick it up . . . Pick it up . . . May, are you there?'

He was still pleading into the phone when he turned to see his mother approaching him. 'Come along, Bunt.'

She was at his elbow, and there was a Chinese man on either side of her. They were as tall and as solid as Hung, with flat bony faces and military haircuts.

Bunt said, 'She won't pick up the phone.'

'Oh?' his mother said and seemed unconcerned. Then, 'I shouldn't worry.'

'If she's not there, where could she possibly be?'

'How should I know?' his mother said peevishly.

'Mum, we can't leave her,' Bunt said in a pleading voice.

But his mother had gripped his arm and she was tugging him to the door.

'Why isn't she answering?'

Now the two Chinese men were just behind them and hurrying them forward to the entrance of the restaurant, the gold-painted moon gate.

'I told her I'd pick her up,' Bunt said. 'She said she'd be waiting.' One of the Chinese men punched him in the small of his back. 'Pardon!'

Many times at Imperial Stitching employees had been recommended by Cheung for dismissal; and Bunt had authorized them. Now and then the person, usually the men, returned and made a fuss – stood on the street and yelled obscenities at the windows; crept into the building and grappled with Mr Woo. But it was Bunt they wanted to see, so that they could insult him. A few had reached the eighth floor and it had always been horrible, the raging indignant man causing a commotion.

'See him out,' Bunt would say, and the man would be propelled like a bundle down the stairs and into the street.

That was how Bunt felt now, like a sacked employee. Almost without moving his legs he was being whisked out of the restaurant. He could not understand why his mother had not objected.

'This car is yours,' Monty was saying. Somehow he had materialized outside the restaurant.

Bunt said, 'There is something you have to know. Wait!'

He had seen those humiliated employees shoe-horned into taxis and sent off in just this way. He was standing next to the car with his mother, and then a man was pressing his head and the next instant they were inside, jammed between the two Chinese guards. Bunt saw Hung standing on the sidewalk in front of the restaurant, working a toothpick around his mouth, his hand cupped for delicacy. Still the man darted the thing at his teeth as the car started up. He followed it with his eyes for a few seconds, no more, and then turned away and conferred with a man next to him. Bunt understood that as far as Hung was concerned he did not exist.

Monty was in the front seat, sitting sideways, his elbow propped on the back-rest.

'We have nothing,' Bunt said. 'No baggage – nothing.'

'You're not short of a bob or two,' Monty said with undisguised contempt.

He meant the million pounds, but Bunt was thinking only of Mei-ping. Why had she not answered the phone?

'Mum, I'm worried,' Bunt said.

Betty took hold of his hot hand and said, 'Oh, she'll be along.' She seemed so sure. She gripped his hand harder. 'If we don't leave now, there's no deal. There won't be any money. And that's not the half of it. You heard him.'

Bunt screamed, 'Take a left!'

The command came with such conviction that the driver

reacted instantly and they were traveling down Waterloo Road at great speed.

Monty tapped the driver's shoulder and said, 'Kai Tek is the other way, Alex.'

'Boss?' the driver said.

'Alex is confused,' Monty said.

'I have to get something at the factory. It won't take a minute.'

Bunt leaned forward and spoke so urgently that the driver listened and responded. Imperial Stitching wasn't far – the roof sign was already in sight. Bunt gave the driver directions, and the Sunday traffic was so light that they arrived at the front door while Monty was still protesting.

Even before the car came to a complete stop, Bunt was out of the car, struggling with the lock on the factory door. There was something in the look of the building, a blankness in the windows reflecting the sky, that told him it was empty. He pushed inside and, too impatient to wait for the elevator, he hurried up the stairs, his feet clattering, all the while shouting, 'Mei-ping!' Hoisting himself upwards using the handrail, he went from landing to landing, floor to floor, Shipping, Labels, Storage, Packing, Stitching, Cutting, the old underwear floor – now closed – and finally Executive Offices, calling 'Mei-ping!'

There was no sign that Mei-ping was there, that she had ever been there, only emptiness and immobility and motionless dust, stilled machines and silenced activity, that made the factory seem haunted by the ghosts of departed workers, a place of bones. That, and residue. A faint vibration lingered in the air, like the echo after a tremendous sound has been struck from a simple instrument, as though he was hearing the last audible whimper from the thunder of a gong.

Feeling that the small sound was slipping away, Bunt

screamed Mei-ping's name, and became terrified when it too diminished to a faint echo among all the indifferent machines. And then, slowly, he descended the stairs.

'Mum,' Bunt said in the car. He wanted to weep.

'Pull yourself together, Neville,' Monty said.

They were at the Kai Tek entrance, gliding up the ramp. Monty was chatting confidently about the future, the new airport on the western side of Kowloon, the new road and fly-over, the reclaimed land, the massive investment – *Next year, next year*, he said. *Next year*.

'I'll take care of everything,' he said.

Bunt had gone weak. At the check-in desk he had his cellular phone open and he was pleading into it, still imploring it, calling her apartment, calling the factory; and again at the security check, and on the jet-way; and after they boarded, in his seat, still pleading, *Pick up the phone, May!*

'I expect something came up,' Betty said. She had a gin and tonic in one hand and the fingers of the other scratched in her dish of warmed mixed nuts. 'I've got no more bally almonds.'

They were in the air. Side by side in the sharply accelerating plane they felt themselves swaying this way and that over the city and were soon being thumped by clouds.

'Maybe she changed her mind,' Betty said.

Why was she so sure, why no sentiment or hesitation, why had she not questioned that sinister detail of Mr Chuck's demise? Nothing, it seemed, had really surprised her.

Bunt was numb. He was sick, his stomach distended with fear, the terror that was no different from the worst runny tummy.

He whimpered but was almost unintelligible. He was holding his cellular phone. He was trying to say, 'Mei-ping.'

In and out of the dense clouds he saw the city in a dusty

twilight in which Kowloon Tong and all its lighted signs was a massive grid of red streets. Then the plane cruised into a cloudscape of whiteness, like a sea of foam, a limitless Arctic.

'Mum,' he said again, feeling like an infant. 'Did you say anything to Mr Hung?'

His mother's teeth always seemed to slip out of alignment when she was untruthful, and though she had not yet said a word, she was chewing her teeth, seeming to right them.

'We're well out of it,' she finally said. She was smiling. Why? 'You'll find someone else. It's true. They all look alike.' Then she lowered her voice because she saw a Chinese woman in a uniform coming down the aisle. 'Chinky-Chonks.'

Tottering slightly in the banking plane, the flight attendant said to Bunt, 'Do you want to turn that off for me?'

Working his thumb into the power switch, Bunt pressed and watched the lights blink, and then fail, and the window faded and the little thing died in his hand with a gulp like a small peep of protest.

SIXTEEN

All of Kowloon Tong trembled as the wrecking ball swung sideways from the crane, hit the sign *Imperial Stitching* and punched it from the roof of the building. The sign shattered as it fell. On the next swing a corner of the top floor went, shaped like a wedge of cake but made of brick. It came apart in a dumping of single bricks as it dropped to the ground. The solid hit on the rest of that floor exposed Miss Liu's office, Lily's cubicle, Mr Cheung's office, the lavatory, the interior of Bunt's suite. The floor was soon on the ground, in pieces. Still the wrecking ball swung, smacking the yielding brick. By degrees the cutting floor, the old underwear floor, Stitching, Packing, Storage, Labels, Shipping, all collapsed in a shower of dust and bricks. It was an old building. It went fast, many of the former employees watched, and some of them wept – wept harder than when they had been fired, just a week before; harder than they had at Mr Chuck's funeral.

No one spoke Mr Hung's name. It seemed dangerous to do so. In any case, he was not present for the demolition.

It was a hot day in late May, the air thick with this morning's evaporated downpour, and the dust was vile, like another wicked aspect of the humidity.

And so it went on, the wrecking ball swinging back and forth, the dumb pockmarked thing suspended from a greasy cable that was worked by a small Chinese man in the dented cab of a Chinese crane. The ball brought down the old building and all its brackets and ornaments, its bricks, its beams, its red doors, its mirrors, its sewing-machines – the parts of Imperial Stitching that represented the Five Elements and held the whole enterprise in balance: Earth, Wood, Fire, Water, Metal.

Soon everything that had been standing lay buried, and the Hong Kong people watching, sensing the *Ch'i* whirling like gas, and feeling exposed and conspicuous with the building gone, tucked their heads down and hurried away. Then the site was empty, just broken stones, with the junked and rubbly look of reclaimed land, and sitting on it was the long-necked crane, like a green dragon with a toy in its mouth.

READ MORE IN PENGUIN

In every corner of the world, on every subject under the sun, Penguin represents quality and variety – the very best in publishing today.

For complete information about books available from Penguin – including Puffins, Penguin Classics and Arkana – and how to order them, write to us at the appropriate address below. Please note that for copyright reasons the selection of books varies from country to country.

In the United Kingdom: Please write to *Dept. EP, Penguin Books Ltd, Bath Road, Harmondsworth, West Drayton, Middlesex UB7 0DA*

In the United States: Please write to *Consumer Sales, Penguin Putnam Inc., P.O. Box 999, Dept. 17109, Bergenfield, New Jersey 07621-0120.* VISA and MasterCard holders call 1-800-253-6476 to order Penguin titles

In Canada: Please write to *Penguin Books Canada Ltd, 10 Alcorn Avenue, Suite 300, Toronto, Ontario M4V 3B2*

In Australia: Please write to *Penguin Books Australia Ltd, P.O. Box 257, Ringwood, Victoria 3134*

In New Zealand: Please write to *Penguin Books (NZ) Ltd, Private Bag 102902, North Shore Mail Centre, Auckland 10*

In India: Please write to *Penguin Books India Pvt Ltd, 210 Chiranjiv Tower, 43 Nehru Place, New Delhi 110 019*

In the Netherlands: Please write to *Penguin Books Netherlands bv, Postbus 3507, NL-1001 AH Amsterdam*

In Germany: Please write to *Penguin Books Deutschland GmbH, Metzlerstrasse 26, 60594 Frankfurt am Main*

In Spain: Please write to *Penguin Books S. A., Bravo Murillo 19, 1° B, 28015 Madrid*

In Italy: Please write to *Penguin Italia s.r.l., Via Benedetto Croce 2, 20094 Corsico, Milano*

In France: Please write to *Penguin France, Le Carré Wilson, 62 rue Benjamin Baillaud, 31500 Toulouse*

In Japan: Please write to *Penguin Books Japan Ltd, Kaneko Building, 2-3-25 Koraku, Bunkyo-Ku, Tokyo 112*

In South Africa: Please write to *Penguin Books South Africa (Pty) Ltd, Private Bag X14, Parkview, 2122 Johannesburg*

BY THE SAME AUTHOR

A selection

My Other Life

'A book about doubt and double identity. Its narrator, Paul Theroux, is a man in the middle of a crack-up – a husband who loses his wife; a traveller who goes off the rails; a novelist who stops writing; a self-seeker who can find himself only in aliases ... It's one man's life, but Everyman's crisis. It seems honest. Even if it isn't honest, it's true' – *Independent on Sunday*

My Secret History

'Nothing on the shelf has quite prepared the reader for *My Secret History* ... Parent saunters into the book aged fifteen, shouldering a .22 Mossberg rifle as earlier, more innocent American heroes used to tote a fishing pole. In his pocket is a paperback translation of Dante's *Inferno* ... He is a creature of naked and unquenchable ego, greedy for sex, money, experience, *another life* ... Wickedly addictive' – *Observer*

The Family Arsenal

Paul Theroux's novel of violence, in the tradition of *Brighton Rock*, is set in the grimy decay of south-east London.

'Brilliant and haunting ... the ingenuities of the plot, the London setting ... the trapped and interwoven people, and the balefully witty observation, have an undistracted force' – *Observer*

Picture Palace

For over fifty years Maude Coffin Pratt has levelled her 'third eye' at the beautiful, obscure and obscene, and at the private places and public parts of the famous, from Gertrude Stein to Graham Greene. At her retrospective exhibition her life, measured by camera spools, is rolled out for inspection, except for the frame that really mattered – the exposure that should have been there, but wasn't.

'Maude's voice, harsh, coarse, and yet surprisingly innocent, remains in the ear long after the book has been put down' – *The Times*

BY THE SAME AUTHOR

A selection

The Mosquito Coast

Allie Fox was going to re-create the world. Abominating the cops, crooks, scavengers and funny-bunnies of the twentieth century, he abandons civilization and takes his family to live in the Honduran jungle. There his tortured, quixotic genius keeps them alive, his hoarse tirades harrying them through a diseased and dirty Eden towards unimaginable darkness and terror.

'An epic of paranoid obsession that swirls the reader headlong to deposit him on a black mudbank of horror' – *Guardian*

'An adventure story of the most exemplary kind ... A work of genuine inspiration, intensely realized' – *New York Magazine*

The Black House

A reign of terror begins for Alfred and Emma Munday when they take their failing marriage to the solace of an old country house. There, in the peace and quiet of the Dorset countryside, a strange and beautiful apparition enters their life, disrupts it ... creates a fatal triangle of fear, fantasy and eroticism.

'Theroux skilfully brings out the strangeness, even menace, lurking beneath the homely and familiar ... beautifully written' – *Sunday Telegraph*

The Collected Stories

'Theroux makes and remakes his own world ... throughout this shimmering, kaleidoscopic and very entertaining collection ... The smell, sound, sight of his scenes is always strong, even pungent; and, even more, his dialogue is powerfully but also effortlessly accurate' – Anthony Thwaite in the *Sunday Telegraph*

'A book of many and varied pleasures; to read it is to feel alert, curious, adventurous' – Sylvia Brownrigg in the *Observer*

Kowloon Tong is also available as a Penguin Audiobook read by Martin Jarvis